Because of the Night

Rue L'Hommedieu

Printed in the United States of America

Paperback ISBN: 978-1-958714-06-5
Ebook ISBN: 978-1-958714-08-9
Hardcover ISBN: 978-1-958714-07-2

Library of Congress Control Number: 2022945008

CHICAGO · NEW YORK · PARIS · ROME
Muse Literary
3319 N. Cicero Avenue
Chicago IL 60641-9998

Contents

To Patricia, Hazel, and Constance L'Hommedieu. Life connects us wisely—by matching one person's strength to another person's weakness.

And, to all who believe they don't fit-in because they're different. Just remember—we are *all* different.

This book is for you…

"Within this crazy ride of life, our differences should never divide us. So, buckle-up sweethearts, we're all in it together."
—Rue L'Hommedieu.

CHAPTER 1

CAUTION: SLIPPERY. WHEN. WET.

"*Icky—gimme back my sun!*"

Kiffer's whisper strains as he tries not to disturb the short-fused guy we call Dad.

Even if my Minnie Mouse clock says 7:00 p.m. and it's still light outside, the town's newspaper presses keep our poor ole dad chained to a strict bedtime. Hearing those faint rumbles from the room next door, it's our tip-off that his nightly routine has started.

"Now, Icky, or I'm . . ." Kiffer's voice deepens as he pushes hard on his threat to make it sound less of a bluff. "If you don't give it back, I'm—I'm gonna tell Mom."

"So what! She won't do nothing."

We both know the truth. Dad says, "It's just a sad mood called *the blues*." But trust me here, I've looked. Mom's color never changes. Not ever.

I lock eyes with my humorless brother. I'll admit, for some reason, the thought of Kiffer advertising our fight tonight made me hesitate for two seconds. But nope—time's up. My brain switches gears and changes direction, again. Like the beam of a spotlight pushing off its target to begin a wide search for a new place to shine. Gramp used to say, "Don't worry; your ability to tune out, detach, and move on, it's a super power." Not sure if Gramp's theory on this is true. I'll stick with the spotlight explanation.

Facing each other like gunslingers in a standoff at the O.K. Corral, we must look ridiculous: Kiffer doing his best evil stare-down, me with one eyebrow raised high above a devilish grin. I shouldn't enjoy watching my parents' smarty-pants golden boy squint with rage, but as his competitive twin sister, I can't help myself. I so enjoy it.

"Go ahead," I say. "Tell her, ... don't . . . care."

I squeeze the ball so hard my rough tomboy nails press jagged marks into my palm. It's only the dumb sun from his constellation mobile, I think. His stupid *last year's* science project. Besides it's finders keepers, right?

While Kiffer stares at me, his eyelids do their typical Morse Code blinking. The muscles in his tight frown melt into a smirk—and here he goes, thinking he's found my weakness.

It's almost sad how often he misreads me. But then again, most people do.

My face puckers as Kiffer curls his bottom lip into a menacing smile.

"Icky . . . Icky," he squeezes out.

Sometimes, nicknames can be painful. Unfair is more like it. With a hard name like Christopher, my brother became *Kiff-ferfer*, Kiffer for short. And when Kiffer swore he couldn't—or wouldn't, most likely—pronounce his Vs, I became Icky. Totally. Not. Fair!

Unfolding my bandaged fingers, evidence from a triumphant bus war fought earlier today, I spread my hand wide and look at this dumb yellow ball. Part of me knows I should be good and just hand it over. But no one—and I mean no one—gets away with calling me a "spaz." Not even Kiffer. And besides, he didn't even ask me nicely.

So instead, I squeeze the ball tight and bolt toward the bathroom. Kiffer leans to one side, attempting an interception. I lean harder and faster to the other and zoom right past him, trying not to pound too loudly on our new avocado-green carpet. Mom brags it's the new chic "it" color for the 1960s.

I say it's the new "vom-it" color. But what do I know? I'm just an easily distracted ten-year-old girl.

Kiffer's forehead wrinkles as he pulls back his arm and realizes he only grabbed thin air. He might be a smart kid—very smart—but he's not too fast.

Kiffer loves to boast to anyone who'll listen: "Higher-than-average IQ—I was tested!"

It's true, and I'll be the first to say his insanely high score is spot-on. I asked Kiffer once, "How heavy is Dad's car?" I was flabbergasted that he didn't know, but he studied for days—obsessed is more like it—then walked up to me casual-like and rattled off, "1955 Packard, four-thousand two-hundred, blah-blah, three-fifty-two cubic . . ."

I tuned him out, of course, while he spat out a hundred more stupid facts no one would ever want to know, especially me.

Kiffer's way too serious about . . . well, everything. Reminds me of Mom's silly soap opera, the one where a mad scientist saves the world by analyzing secret data in some hidden underground lab. He's so . . . annoying.

Reaching the bathroom, I step through and safely lock the door handle behind me. Kiffer slams into the outside of the door. His skin scrapes against the painted wood, making it vibrate as he slides down into a heap on the hallway floor.

This I gotta see.

Bending down, I ignore the yucky smell of Mom's pine floor cleaner, press my cheek against the linoleum and focus one eye through the gap under the door. Yep, just as I thought. There's Kiffer, flat on his back, directly under the doorknob. He bangs his fist against the carpet in protest, grumbling distorted words through his T-shirt, which is now all bunched up under his armpits.

Hey, Kiffer—how's the higher IQ working for ya now?

This last thought makes me smile. But something within me still feels wrong. Why did this crazy world make us complete opposites? Kiffer's the calm, smarty-pants golden boy. I'm the fidgety stubborn mule with the attention span of a gnat.

But I'm almost as smart.

Yes, I was tested too. I only get retested yearly, which is ridiculous if you ask me. So what if ants are in my pants, my train of thought constantly derails, and I don't understand most grownup things? Duh—I'm a kid! This is no proof I'm somewhere between slow-to-mature and tension-deficit-something-something. Just because someone wears a doctor's white coat doesn't mean they know everything about me.

Kiffer's chest rises as he sucks in a deep breath, creating the perfect time for me to blast a few evil laughs under the door. Now, most of his options have run out. He turns his head, aiming his desperate voice through the same gap beneath the door.

"Give me back my sun . . . now," he whines.

Our single bulging eyes meet under the door. I spring to my feet and back away. Closing the commode lid, I sit, flattening the yarn design on Mom's beloved crocheted toilet cover. Gripping the ball tight, I smile and lean back against the tank. Man, that was close. It's not easy for me to focus and have a plan to succeed, so winning at something against Kiffer just doesn't happen often.

Let's be real; the best part of this small victory is that I don't even *need* his stupid ball. Sometimes, you want what your brother wants. And if it aggravates Mr. Smarty Pants, all the better.

"*Arrr-grumf*," Kiffer grunts as he stands up. The ends of my smile relax as I hear *swish-thump, swish-thump-thump* moving down the hallway toward our bedroom. Yes, "our bedroom." I didn't mind giving up my room to sweet Gramp after his stroke or admitting I'm the only one shrimpy enough to fit in Kiffer's bottom bunk. The real problem is having to share a room with Mr. Smarty Pants. Ugh.

I hear Kiffer's moccasin slippers, imagine that smell of burnt leather, and see his feet rubbing rough on the carpet as he heads back toward the locked bathroom. Suddenly, brown nylon hair is swishing back and forth under the door—teasing proof he's found my favorite doll. He threatens her with bodily harm if I don't exchange it for his precious sun ball.

Poor Kiffer, this time you've failed—big-time. That Barbie you've picked—my favorite? You're way off! In fact, I don't normally like dolls. Never have. But, for some weird reason, there's this blonde Ponytail Barbie. She's my one and only prized possession—and she's buried deep inside Kiffer's unopened closet, nice and safe.

"Never in a million-gazillion years," I say, raising one side of my snarled lip.

A sharp *snap* comes from some part of the doll's anatomy.

No—he did not! How dare he break something of mine. He leaves me with no other choice. I jump to my feet and grab the toilet lid so hard it pulls off the crocheted cover, which slides out between my fingers and lands in a wad on the floor.

Wham! The bare lid slams back down.

"Dang it!" I yell and fling it back open.

Wham! It crashes against the porcelain tank again. I grip the ball between my fingers, snap my wrist, and—with a satisfying *ker-plop*—toss in the ball.

Kiffer has problems with germs, different foods touching on his plate, and a few other quirks. So, this is way up at the top of the list of the worst things to do to him. Ah, sweet revenge.

After hearing this unsanitary ball bath, Kiffer inhales a loud, wet snort, which is as ugly a sound as you'd imagine. In the toilet, this spongy rubber ball refuses to sink. It bounces up and down like a fish bobber on a little tsunami.

"No!" Kiffer howls from the other side of the bathroom door.

My pre-spanking radar goes into autopilot. It scans to see if this higher volume activated Dad. After a pause so silent it is deafening, a "Whew!" rises on both sides of the bathroom door before the sibling fight continues.

"Yeah, just you wait," Kiffer says. "I'll be right back."

Oh, boy—that didn't sound good. More *swish-thumps* head toward our bedroom. The sharp opening creak of his closet door cuts through the air. Did he remember?

That creak alarm—it's the first layer of protection to my most valued treasure, my mint-condition Ponytail Barbie, kept in its original box. With no bow or card, the doll was left on my bed the morning of my eighth birthday. What makes this doll, of all my things, so important? I'm not sure. But it is.

I flinch at the sound of him rummaging deep into the closet, then hear the *click* of the latch to my doll case. Oh, crapola. He *did* remember! As slower thumps pound the carpet, I can picture him marching back, all proud, with his lips turned up like a notorious villain.

When his footsteps stop, two shadows appear under the bathroom door.

"Yep. You . . . just . . . wait," he says.

With no time to react, I hear the crinkle sounds of my helpless Barbie being taken out of her plastic wrap. I'm shocked. Kiffer usually doesn't lose his patience like me. My mouth goes dry while a stampede races beneath my belly button. I can't even move. Not a single muscle.

With his anger still boiling, Kiffer does the stupidest thing—ever. He's not even gonna wait for my answer to his new threat. I hear the sickening break of the Barbie's plastic body. Her murdered corpse drops to the floor, projecting additional shadows under the door.

Well, *now* he's pushed me too far.

Reaching over, I press down on the chrome handle and s*wish*—say goodbye, yellow sun.

Come on, Kiffer—whatcha think I was gonna do?

The stubborn ball floats on top of the swirling water like a surfer on the crest of a mighty wave.

"No!" Kiffer's shriek echoes between the tiled walls of the bathroom, so loud I bet every person in China heard it.

The ball dances about as the waves crash into the center. Then, finally, it disappears with the remaining water. Strange gurgling sounds rumble under my feet.

Okay. I may not have thought this through.

I stare wide-eyed as the empty bowl gradually refills, overfills, and overflows. The water slides down the porcelain base toward my feet and engulfs the crocheted cover. I slowly back up until my shoulders press against the bathroom door. The piney smell of the clean floors mixed with bleach fills the room.

"Uh oh," I say, the words sorta dribbling out of my mouth.

It's time to flee the scene of the crime. My hands paw at the knob as I unlock the door and step into the hall. Then a new kind of rumbling sound rises, coming from our parents' room, cutting the still air.

Like deer in headlights, Kiffer and I stand frozen and look at each other hopelessly. Our parents' bedroom door bangs open. Through the darkened doorway, wearing flannel sleeping pants, Dad lumbers out with a toothbrush hanging on for dear life from his gaping mouth.

Oh, yes. My brother and I now know this battle. It's so over.

Our father has two moods—or extremes, as I like to call them. One is a class clown, funnier than Jerry Lewis. The other is the hateful Mr. Potter from *It's a Wonderful Life.* As Dad stands with his arms crossed, we watch his enraged face turn beet red. It's not hard to tell which mood is winning tonight.

"What the—what's going on here?" Dad says. Toothpaste sprays everywhere.

The entire house goes silent. This includes Mom's normal clanking noises in the kitchen, where she's cleaning the dinner dishes.

Crapola, now everyone's going to get involved.

I prepare for the worst and glance over my shoulder toward downstairs. Here it comes.

With many kitchen towels in hand, Mom rushes up the stairs, grumbling random complaints.

"Every night, every . . . night, why can't I just have—"

Mom passes by, bumping me slightly with her hip like I'm not even there. For a moment, I get a whiff of tonight's roasted chicken and her after-dinner cigarette, tailgating on her. And in case you're wondering—these smells *do not* mix well.

She follows the water streaming from ground zero, dropping towels as she goes, then jiggles the handle to stop the tank from overflowing. When she sees her beloved lid cover soaked flat to the floor, her fingers flare, then clench. Her shoulders sag in unison with her head, just like a stringed puppet.

"Can't . . . one night . . . without . . . tired of this . . ."

Her broken words somehow match her shattered glare. As her shoes squish on the soaked towels, she shoots a fiery glance toward all of us.

She locks eyes with Kiffer. "Straight to bed," she mutters, with control that sounds almost painful.

Mom flashes Dad a disgusted smirk, ricochets it to me, then begins sopping up the water.

These days, she pretty much ignores me. Mom used to notice me. Like the time when she stayed up all night sewing us matching mother-daughter field trip outfits. That was before the Ponytail Barbie showed up. Or not. Anyway, it's too long ago to remember, let alone remember what changed it all. But something sure did.

"Christopher—now!" Mom says, puzzled anger plastered across her face.

Kiffer stands there like a perfect marble statue. He jerks awake from his trance, turns, and darts to our room.

Dad gives a low gargled sigh, grabs my ear, and off we go. Don't worry about the ear thing—it's normal. Happens regularly, or at least regularly to me. It's Dad's way of keeping my attention. And here it comes, that familiar ear pain. Starts as a pressured pinch, then a sharp burn settles in. I can fool my ear into believing it's not any worse than when it goes numb after playing outside in the snow, hatless. And you know those squinting wrinkles that happen when you anticipate pain? Mine have all melted away. *See? Told ya. I'm just fine.*

"You! Come with me," Dad says, closing the bathroom door behind us.

Mom is left sopping up the floor, alone. Hard to say if he's hiding me from her or her from me.

As I'm pulled downstairs, Dad's fingers grab a better hold, higher up my ear. That nice smell of roasted chicken is long gone, replaced with the scent of Dad's aftershave mixed with a minty toothpaste.

"What is wrong with you?" he asks. "Scatterbrained, that's what it is. Can't pay attention—to anything. You know Mom can't handle you like this, don't you?"

I feel the banging of answers tumbling inside my head. My sarcastic response must stay inside me: *Yes, Dad. I know, but do you? Do you know what it's like trying to finish a thought when you can't even finish a sentence? Or try to focus straight ahead and your brain would rather zigzag? So yes, Dad. I do know.*

But all I dare to say out loud is, "Yes, Dad."

For maybe a nanosecond, his face hints that he understands. But by the time we reach the coat closet at the bottom of the stairs, his scowling face proves me wrong once again.

As Dad rummages around in the closet for his tool bucket, I should be amazed at the coordination of his one free hand. But instead, I'm already distracted and peer into the kitchen. It looks like a garden threw up everywhere. Its wallpaper is plastered with more vomit green and gaggles of speckled flowers everywhere. Gramp is sitting at the table, staring strangely out the window as if he's listening to someone outside.

Replacing one distraction with another, I look back to the closet just in time to notice Dad's beloved Polaroid camera wobbling dangerously on the edge of the top shelf. His rough searching stops. He throws one last wrench into his overflowing tool bucket and slams the door closed with his shoulder.

Then *ka-bam*, the beloved camera falls, hitting something hard in the closet's darkness. Dad's head drops while his white lips tighten around the forgotten toothbrush. He drags out a long curse word—the one we're not allowed to say.

If I could only disappear, like how the TV turns off at night. The screen shrinks to a flat line, shrivels to a dot in the middle, then vanishes into static. Distracted again, I hear another Kiffer lecture replaying in my head: "When power's cut, stored energy, tubes, *blah-blah* … capacitors drain, picture collapses, *blahhhh*." Oh, ugh.

I can barely hear anything with my ear pinned closed in Dad's grip. Of course, I hear each word of "I'm so disappointed in you," as clear as a bell.

It's so unfair. How does everything become my fault?

My ear gets pinched a little harder as minty foam sprays out with every shouted word. *My gosh, how much toothpaste did he use?*

Yep, these kinds of random thoughts seem to take over, especially after I mess up. It makes it impossible for me to focus. It sabotages me. A lot.

They say my strong inability to pay attention keeps me from learning much after mistakes. So, now you know why my skill to tune out, detach, and move on is my superpower.

"Why's it so hard for you to behave?" Dad says.

I know questions directed toward me usually aren't, well, questions. And his annoyed face confirms this one's definitely not.

We make it to the tiny room under the stairs. In this plumbing closet, all the house's water pipes connect and where the last pipe trap is located. The first-time hearing about those traps, I pictured our pipes full of tiny mouse traps with rodents scampering inside them.

We step inside the closet. Finally, he releases my ear.

"Just stand there," Dad says.

He drops the bucket, which makes a loud *boom* as it hits the floor. Inside this cramped room, the strong forest smell from the stairs' pine beams and wood floorboards suggests I'm in the center of a giant, hollowed-out tree.

Dad takes a deep breath, like an exhausted doctor preparing for grueling surgery on one of Mom's soap operas.

And so begins the pipe operation: dun—dun—DUN! *Good gravy, I really must stop watching Mom's silly soap operas!*

Dad's wrench clanks on the metal pipes, water and curses flying every which way. The sun-ball suddenly pops free, along with a small toy soldier from some previous sibling battle.

Dad throws them both out on the wet floor. His face strains while he tightens the last pipe into place. A drop of sweat rolls down his temple. He raises his forearm, smearing it back across his brow. As he turns to throw the wrench into the bucket, his damp socks slip on the wet boards. He hits his elbow hard on a wall brace but somehow avoids a complete fall. His pale lips pucker and clench together.

Don't believe what they say—that bone in the elbow, it's not so funny.

In a split second, my thoughts switch again. I better sidetrack Dad—and fast. Bending down cool-like, I pick up the wet ball and put on my helpless cutie-pie look. Sometimes, this can cancel out a spanking that's on the way.

Oh, yeah—I've still got it! Dad's frown softens as he rubs his elbow and steps outside the closet, leaving the door wide open. I follow. He looks around the living room, confused.

"Where's your mom?" he asks.

Before I can answer him, as if I'd have an answer, he grabs the corduroy strap to my overalls and pulls me along behind him. At least the ear gets a break.

Dad stops us near the front door and peers into the kitchen. His jaw muscles bulge as we watch Mom slam the refrigerator and cabinet doors while she finishes the dishes.

Mom's emotions can't handle stress, no matter how small. That's just how it is. She's got three basic reactions to it:

No. 1: Bursts of anger.

No. 2: Tears.

No. 3: (Mom's personal favorite) Withdrawal into some secret world that none of us can be a part of.

Tonight, she appears stuck at No. 1.

Dad's face goes limp while he groans something so unusual. "You're gonna help me tonight," he says, stretching out a deep sigh.

I'm super-duper flabbergasted! I don't care how much he dreaded saying those words—or just said them to avoid dealing with Mom—he said them, and my ears heard them.

My heart jumps inside my chest as if bouncing on a mini trampoline. For the first time, I'm going to be Dad's helper. With the crucial flush testing, no less.

Wow—oh, wow! *Okay, I might have said that out loud.*

"Go upstairs and just stand there," Dad says. "Don't do anything. Not a thing till I tell you to."

He disappears back under the staircase.

"Okay, okay, okay!" I say and take off.

Running past the kitchen doorway, I turn to head up the stairs, squeezing the wet ball so tight water droplets ooze out between my fingers.

I'm so thrilled at this new trusted duty I accidentally cut in front of Gramp, who is now struggling to navigate from the kitchen to the living room.

My sweet Gramp. After his stroke, he retired from the DOT signage department and had to move in with us. Now he spends much of his day alone, sitting by the kitchen window. Mom says he's just sad because of his disabilities. I say—not as often or as loud—he's sad living in this messed-up family. Okay, okay. It's possible we're both right.

"Caution. Slippery. When. Wet," Gramp says, glancing at my hand.

Nowadays, only road-sign words come out when he speaks. To understand what he's trying to say, you have to pay close attention to each word.

Yep, you got it—not my strongest talent.

"Not now, Gramp. I'm Dad's helper tonight!" I blurt out respectfully and fly up the stairs, ignoring his warning.

"Only do what Dad says to do. Only what he says to do."

I tell myself over and over. This should be so simple. But if you think even someone like me couldn't mess this up, you'd be so wrong.

After reaching the top of the stairs, I peer into our shared bedroom. Oh no, he . . . did . . . *not.*

There's Kiffer, sound asleep, and he's wrapped tight in *my* Kimba the Lion blanket.

My face twists up in a tight wad as I start planning my revenge, rubbing my chin like an evil villainess. *Let's see . . . if I fling this wet ball of germs right between his eyes, he'll wake up all grossed out. It'll be hilarious. Mwahaha.*

Yep—but nope, I must focus.

It takes all my strength to pull my stare off my brother, the blanket thief, and force my legs to keep walking.

The floors are still damp as I step back into the clean bathroom. The lid cover hangs on the towel rack, stretched out and dripping. Mom is so determined to use that ugly old thing. I won't lie—I hope it's ruined.

I'm panting with excitement. Thoughts burst across my brain like shooting stars. I won't be spanked tonight— not if I'm a great helper and all. With my head held high, I stand tall beside the tank and look toward the hallway.

A half-smile covers my face. Right this minute, my life feels dang good. Kiffer's in bed, and I'm the lucky one here being Dad's helper. Somehow, even the carpet doesn't look so, well, vomit-green anymore. A full-on smile now takes over as I push out my chest and wait for his next order.

"All right," I hear from downstairs, "try it again!"

"Okay!" I yell back.

This is way too awesome.

Normally, when my day tumbles downhill the way it did tonight, I'd be sent straight to bed. But not this time.

A tingle starts inside my stomach, like the first time I rode my bike without training wheels. I shake with joy as my mind races. Just think, I may even win Dad's "Best Helper of the Year" award.

But in true Icky form, things take a terrible turn.

Have you ever done something without thinking, then right away yelled at yourself, "What on Earth made me do this?" I mean, come on—this should have been the easiest part of my job.

But no.

With my stellar non-thinking reflexes, I step in closer, toss the ball in, and *swish*—goodbye yellow sun ball. Again.

All right, there I go again. All common sense just—*poof!*—vanished. Has Mom, Dad's regular flush tester, ever gotten over-excited and made this kind of mistake?

And more importantly, can I still get an award?

The correct answers: *no*, Mom has never . . . and *no,* I will remain award-less tonight.

It's *so* that time to reposition my spotlight—to tune out, detach, and move on.

CHAPTER 2

RUNAWAY. TRUCK. RAMP.

You'd think, by now, my two frustrated parents should know I have no acceptable answers to: "How can you be so…?" and "Why can't you be…?" But they keep asking anyway.

With sweaty hands clasped behind my back, I try my best to stand still while they finish the inquisition. They soon become fed up with my silence and finally send me to bed.

My entire body tightens. If things had been explained to me better, maybe I wouldn't make so many bad decisions like this. Then I could fit in better with my family. If only I could slow down my thoughts and focus like Kiffer does. My gramp used to help me with this. He'd hold both my hands and make me count backward from ten.

I miss the old Gramp.

While I'm banished to my bottom bunk, Mom is re-enlisted as Dad's helper. In random spurts, screams shoot back and forth between them for the entire re-de-clogging process.

Which, yes—now I know *all* the "correct" steps.

The stairs creak one by one as someone treks up. The sound of hard slip-on scuffs clinks on the wet bathroom floor, revealing the better helper is at her post. Thanks a lot, Mom.

"Come on—let's go!" Mom yells from the bathroom.

Dad starts his command, "Okay ..."

Then there's a slipping *screech* with a *boom* rising from beneath the stairs.

Oh boy—the toy soldier? I jolt up so quickly that the top of my head hits the upper bunk.

"Ouchy," I yelp and fall back into the pillow.

I roll out sideways and land on my feet in one motion. With a palm pressed against my throbbing forehead, I cup my ear to the door. From under the staircase, Dad curses away. I hide behind closed eyes and soundless lips. Nope, this is not good.

"Okay—now!" he barks up again from the closet.

Swish! The sound of water gushing down the pipes is followed by the tank's refilling hiss. The house goes dead quiet. Then, like the slow beat of a sad old elephant's gait, heavier steps plod up the stairs. *Wham*, our parents' bedroom door slams shut.

My eyes open wider. I jerk back and look across the room at Kiffer.

Like a moth in a cocoon, he's still wrapped up tight in my Kimba blanket, oblivious to the outside world. As I rub my throbbing forehead, that stampede in my belly has now traveled to my head. This is totally not fair. At all.

Mom's shoe tapping continues as she cleans the

bathroom for the second time tonight. After a minute of stillness, the clank of Mom's rings hit the bedroom doorknob. I leap toward the bed, slide across the sheets, and hit the hard wall on the other side. One of my bandages peels off and disappears between the wall and mattress.

The bedroom door opens. Mom takes a few steps in, then turns her face toward the window. Her pale profile shows absolutely no emotion.

Slow moaning words seep out of her as she gazes out the window. "Don't know what to do with you . . . you can't sit still, fidget all the time, can't whisper, you scream." Her face turns red as she inhales a deep, slow breath. "And to listen? Forget about it. Just like at Grandma's funeral when you . . . oh, I just give up."

Complaints like this the closest thing to a conversation she has with me. Instead of dealing with life on Earth with us, she lives most of the time alone, somewhere inside her head. Sometimes I'll catch Mom smiling as she cooks her infamous spaghetti dinner. Or, when conditions are just right, she'll sit on the porch humming with the radio while she draws the most magnificent horse pictures you've ever seen. But to hope her happy thoughts are ever about me . . . not hardly.

I just don't get it; why can't Mom just talk to me?

I mean . . . most afternoons after school, she'll ask Kiffer, "How was your day?" and "Did you eat all your lunch today?"

But with me: nothing.

Normally I know to let this dark moment pass, an unspoken lesson learned since forever. The real trick is to bite your tongue and wait. She'll defuse herself with one verbal finale, then retreat into her silent cave.

Yep—biting my tongue, also not high on my list of things I can do successfully.

As the pressure builds inside me, I try my tune-out, move on and detach strategy. But being so close to winning Dad's Best Helper tonight, I'm way too revved up inside.

At this point, I'll take any answer that keeps these racing thoughts from piling up in my head. Can it be because my family doesn't love me? Since Gramp changed, there's no one around here who understands me, that's for sure.

Truth is—even *I* don't understand myself.

My veins feel like they're pumping hot lava. I try again to disconnect from the brewing pressure, but it's not working. It rises inside my chest, passes over my tongue, but stops behind my teeth like they're strong prison bars. I slap my hand against my mouth as if it's something I can physically hold back.

Like Mom, I stare out the window. Why do most days seem to wind up where this one ended? Maybe the answer is out there, in the night, somewhere outside my bedroom window.

My mouth goes dry as one of a gazillion thoughts jam in the middle of my throat. Just when I start to tune out, detach and move on, this ball of words becomes unclogged. In one huge explosion, my teeth, lips, and even my hand can't hold it in any longer—

Shut the front door—"I'm in the wrong family!" I shout.

Oh my gosh—finally! *This* must be the reason why I don't seem to fit in.

"Is that right?"

The crease between Mom's eyebrows goes flat. Her face turns red and blotchy.

"Welcome to the club," she says.

She leans forward like she wants to add more, but instead, she turns and walks silently out of the bedroom.

Okay, Mom is taking this *way* too well. I'm confused.

This fight hit deeper than I usually let them. And really, why am I feeling it at all? That's what the tune out, detach and move on skill is for. It's as if saying, "I'm in the wrong family," unstuck a rusted gate inside my chest and burst it wide open, exposing feelings I didn't even know I had. Relief, fear? Whatever it's called, *something* colossal shifted inside me.

Yep, the right family—that's the answer! If I can find a new one, the *right* one, then I'll get more love and understanding. I'll finally fit in, solving all my problems.

Starting a quest to find my *right* family sounds exciting, but this kind of big adventure will need a big plan. Of course, with me, there's no real planning.

Within minutes, I head downstairs, tightly gripping onto my doll case, hastily filled with injured Barbies and, of course, *my* blanket, suavely yanked off Kiffer. With a pillow pinned hard under my other arm, head held high, I walk defiantly past Mom, who's leaning against the open front door.

"Good luck finding the right family," she says with her arms crossed tightly over her chest. "In case you can't— the front door, it'll be unlocked."

She may have meant that as a helpful hint, but I'm using those words to help fuel the burning fire inside me. I step off our porch and glare out across our giant neighborhood.

Like a huge maze, thousands of neatly lined cookie-cutter homes, all laid out in repeating patterns, spread over half of our entire town. Across the street, the sun is setting behind the houses.

With blinding anger, I face this big world—alone.

I shove my shoulders back and walk down our driveway. All decked out in my best PJs, my cool matching robe hangs stylishly open—well, maybe not so stylish—the cats on my pajama bottoms look faded and backward. That's weird since they're brand new. I scurry out of Mom's view to the other side of Dad's car. Leaning down for a closer look, my entire bottom lip disappears as I suck it inside my mouth. Shut the front door—my pants are on inside out!

Wow—you've got to be kidding me.

I close my eyes tight as my chin drops to my chest. My fingers un-clench the case's handle. With a *clunk*, the case falls to the driveway. I pull on the robe's heavy material, wrapping it tightly to my body. Then I fumble for the flannel ends of the belt and tie a big knot.

I inhale a deep breath and lift my mouth on one side like Elvis. So there—I still look good—totally meant to wear it like this.

Wrapped tight in my thick robe over a warm layer of stubbornness, I feel invincible. I'll show her—bet I won't even have to walk very far. I snatch the case by its handle and continue the mission: to find my *right* family.

Because of my oversized fluffy slippers, my intentional stomping is muffled as I continue to scuff toward the end of the driveway. Right before I reach the slabbed sidewalk, a new thought stops me cold. I must stay within earshot to hear those begging pleas for my return. Yep, makes perfect sense to me.

But no pleas are pled—*if pled is a word*. The only sounds are from a few cold night crickets in the damp grass and the faraway sound of a plane's engine above. Again, another Kiffer lecture plays in my head: "It's not the engine you hear—it is the intake, compression, combustion, and exhaust that produces all the sound."

I look up to the night's sky, do a hard eye roll, and push Kiffer's info dump clean out of my brain. Like I said—the sound of a plane's engine. Take that—Kiffer!

Even with my strong, stubborn confidence, a creepy sense of dread oozes in. *Come on, Vicky—shine your spotlight somewhere else—tune out, detach, and move on.*

Gulping down an empty swallow brings up a drowned sigh from inside my stomach, forming a knot in my throat. Feeling like a misfit within my family is one thing. To be angry, confused, and sad out here feels . . . well, lonely.

I shift my attention to the sidewalk in front of me. As usual, it won't matter for long.

In seconds, I'm happily distracted, fully immersed in that kid superstition: "Step on a crack, break your mother's back." Yep—the attention span of a gnat.

One, two, three, step on a crack. One, two, three, step on a crack. It's not easy, but I manage to time the last critical stomp with a side glance back home. I mean—to my *old* home.

Gramp looks confused and upset as he leans onto the front doorknob for support as Mom spins around, walks past him, and fades into the house's darkness. A glow cuts across the front lawn as a light abruptly turns on in the kitchen. Does Mom not even care about me?

With this last view of home, a weird feeling flows into my arms and legs.

Before I allow any more of this sentimental goopy-gop to sink in, I whip my eyes back to the ground in front of me. Homesickness? Oh, no, no, no; this is not happening!

My mind rewinds, and my chest puffs up with hot air and more stubbornness. As every crack gets its deserved stomp, that growing discomfort inside me calms down.

Like an eerie echo, Gramp's voice strains across the lawn, "Runaway. Truck. Ramp." The quiver in Gramp's words cut through me, making my legs stiffen and go numb. Separating from emotion—for me—is easy. But to be cut off by physical distance, especially from him, is a different story.

Strange, unwelcomed feelings start swirling around me like flies around a garbage can. I must shove them back into whatever hiding place they crawled out of, then start my usual tune out, detach, and move on.

As the racing feelings slow inside me, my soft slippers can't pound the cement hard enough to be called stomping anymore. I must control my thoughts and focus on my mission: to find my *right* family.

By now, all the golden colors in the sky have faded. Dampness seeps into the air. Out from the corner of my eye, a bright light flashes like a speeding sparkler. It hugs the street, zooms to the end of the block, then vanishes. I know it's too cold for fireflies—but there's nothing else it can be. Right?

Still stepping on all the cracks humanly possible, I scuff my way closer toward the first house, the white house belonging to the Garafolas. The Garafolas are a fun, loud Italian family with four kids, all close in age to Kiffer and me. Yes, this makes it the perfect place to start my search. And of all the kids on the block, Kiffer and I play with them the most. Just think—if I join *this* family—I'll already know my new brothers and sisters. See, told you I'm smart.

My steps speed up as I think up reasons why the Garafolas will need a super-duper girl in fuzzy cat slippers. After settling on the best one, I rehearse it out loud—you know, to hear how it great it sounds. "Better to complete your family with an instant potty-trained girl rather than a dumb baby."

Yep, that's perfection right there.

I raise my head high, break into a skip, and head down the Garafolas' driveway. Just think how overjoyed they'll be at becoming my new family. My cheeks stretch wide as I grin and whiz past an identical car to ours.

Those Packard car dealerships must have great clearance sales.

As I step onto their porch, the Garafolas' kitchen phone is ringing. This is great—it means they're still awake.

Reaching on tippy toes, I press their lighted doorbell. It takes forever before anyone comes to the door, but when they do, it's Mrs. Garafola. She's ready for bed: hair rollers in, usual heavy makeup off.

Never seeing Mrs. Garafola's face without all the spackled war paint on before, she's almost unrecognizable—unrecognizable *scary*, that is.

I take a step back. Oh no! Have I gone to the wrong house? My lips gap open like a thermometer is going to be inserted. This new family quest thing—not as easy as I thought.

What if it's not even possible?

Well—that's enough of that, Vicky. Can't let myself even think it—at least not yet.

Mrs. Garafola leans out while opening the door, but only wide enough to allow the porch light to shine on her twisted, confused face. When she finally speaks, it's more of a command than a question.

"What do you want, Vicky—"

Um—yeah—this isn't the warm greeting I was hoping for. Something deep inside me makes a hard U-turn. So, I quickly brief her on the basic facts of my situation and eagerly wait for my new mom's tense face to change into a more loving, *welcome to our family* kind of softness. I mean, after all—this is her *lucky* day!

Mrs. Garafola's half-opened eyes are overloaded with questions. Her face muscles tighten around her puckered lips. "Sorry, we don't need more kids here."

This can't be happening! One of my gazillion thoughts pushes to the front of the line. One terrible, awful thought. Is it me? Is she angry at me? No one else is standing here—so yep, it must be me.

She adds another *sorry,* then pulls her head back inside and closes the door. I sit with my mouth hanging open. If Kiffer could see me now, he'd say something gross like, "You're gonna catch flies like that."

While staring at the closed door only inches from my face, I palm my chin to help close my mouth. I've been so fixed on my journey that I didn't prepare for rejection. After all, they know me, they like me—but they don't want me?

While something is doing flip-flops inside my tummy, a spot between the middle of my eyebrows and nose feels like a jagged crack is being ripped apart. Pressure pulses behind my eyes. My eyelashes dampen with over-filled tears—blurring my view as I look back toward the road. They start popping like water balloons and I do a rare thing; I cry.

Setting my doll case down, I use both hands to lift the fallen pillow and tuck it back under my arm. It's not just the pillow I lost my grip on—I lost something else after hearing Mrs. Garafola's *first* sorry. I don't know exactly what to call it, but I know I don't like it—at all.

I grab my case and turn around. Parts of the gutsy girl who stood here only a few minutes ago have vanished. I miss her already.

The sporadic parked cars and small trees stage quietly under the glow from the streetlights that just flickered on. Stepping off the Garafolas' porch, I walk back toward the sidewalk dragging this heavy, unimaginable rejection with me.

Something doesn't feel right. The lights on our street that make you feel safe at night are now sending beams that puncture through the branches of the trees. They dance and skim off the tops of the parked cars, projecting animated ghostly forms on the sidewalk. Everything, including shadows, is coming alive. Trust me, I'm not the kind of kid that scares easy—not in my neighborhood, that is—but I've got this weird feeling the surrounding darkness is not because of the night. I've only walked two houses away, but the real distance between my old home and me now might as well be as far away as the moon.

I can almost hear Smarty-Pants Kiffer inside my head showing off: "About thirty Earths, or 238,900 space miles away." *Why's there so much room for stupid stuff like this and not for things I need to remember?* Oh—ugh.

My scuffing slows; only half of the cracks get nailed now. Before reaching the next driveway, the Dorsey's, I press my face into the pillow, wiping the drying tears off both cheeks. As a strange kind of sadness builds inside me, my throat feels so thick that I can barely swallow.

Okay. Good time to tune out, detach, and move on. If these yucky feelings could go away, I could focus on the sidewalk and force curls to the ends of my pouting lips.

One, two, three, stomp. One, two, three, stomp.

I nail the final blow on the last crack before turning down the Dorsey's driveway. Mr. and Mrs. Dorsey have two small boys, Jacob and Troy. They're not like the Garafolas, but I guess they'll do. Rumor has it Mrs. Dorsey is going to have another baby. But I want to believe she's just really, really fat. This way, it'll fit perfectly with my next new pitch: "You see, Mrs. Dorsey, this way, you'll be *sure* to get a girl!" Tada! Dad has tried for years to move from the press floor to sales, so he often sputters around the house things like: "What's the sales pitch—the best angle to use?" Never thought his grumbles would be of any help to me. But there ya go, tonight, it did. Twice.

They still could be the *right* family. I step on their front porch. Perching on tippy toes, I mash the lit doorbell and manage to knock over their empty dairy bottles left for the morning milkman to exchange.

Oh man, come on!

Don't know whether it was my repeated doorbell rings or the deafening clank of the crashing bottles that brings Mr. Dorsey to the door. He swings it open so fast that I jump back, releasing my grip again on my poor pillow. Whatever bottles survived from the first bowling round are now toppled over, with one rolling off the porch.

At first, my potential new dad glares down at me like he's sizing me up. Obviously, he was making sure his new daughter was A-OK. Through a grimace, he scans the wreckage around me.

My knees start to shake, and I lose my train of thought—including most of my new sales pitch. Like having stage fright on a theatre stage, my mind screams, "*And . . . you're on!*"

Thankfully, I remember the *most* important part: "This way—you'll be guaranteed a girl." And my inner voice again screams, *"Tada!"*

I stand ready for his gasp of agreement, hoping it's followed by a long emotional hug where joyful tears will for sure be shared. Instead, he has only one word for me: "Sorry." And he practically chuckles it, like if he said anything more, he would burst out laughing.

Starting to hate that "S" word, almost as much as my dumb nickname.

A tiny tremor takes over my chin as I stare at his strange smirk. He leans his head sideways while his body follows it around me and corrals the strewn bottles before stepping back inside.

As the door closes, he throws out that bad "*S*"word one last time. Then, the Dorsey's living room lights go off. A few inner lights of mine flicker off as well.

Oh—man! Maybe I should just give up and head back home. After saying, "I'm with the wrong family" tonight, I thought I'd discovered the perfect answer to why I can't fit in. So, honestly, where *is* all this internal drama oozing from?

Bending over to grab my doll case and a dirty pillow, I make the most adorable loud sigh. It's too bad I'm the only one around to hear it.

I step off the porch. While I head toward the driveway, my lips twist over to one side to aim my voice backward. "Didn't want to be your daughter anyway. So there."

I throw my shoulders back and lift my head high. Probably too high. My foot lands on the round side of the one strayed bottle Mr. Dorsey didn't pick up. It propels out from under my slipper and rockets under his car. Down I go—butt first.

"Mom!" I cry out.

My trusted pillow hits the ground first and cushions the landing. It's a miracle. My dignity is saved—at least for now. It's a funny thing about getting hurt—or a close call to it—automatically, you reach out for your mom. Even with bonds as detached as ours—*who'd of thought, right?*

Crapola! Can't let these feelings be happening to me. Must think spotlight—tune out, detach, and move on. Most definitely.

I slide my legs back under me and struggle to my feet while pulling on the front of my bunched-up robe. I grab the ends and again retie the belt with such force that it knocks the wind out of me.

"*Umf,*" I say. With a soft burp, the last of the air escapes from deep inside my chest. I pucker out my bottom lip as far as humanly possible.

Snatching up my flattened super-pillow and doll case, I head toward the sidewalk. *Not gonna tell him about that bottle under his car either. So—there!*

As I look ahead, an eerie blackness surrounds the glowing edges coming from the streetlights. A strangeness fills the air like the vibration of someone silently whispering in your ear. Even the crickets have gone quiet.

That strong, damp, pond-like smell creeps in again. *Oh boy. Not liking this at all.*

Goose bumps form on the skin of my neck and arms. For the first time tonight, I look over my shoulder for the lurking dangers I'm sure must be all around me now—a drooling monster or a warty witch is not out of the question here.

I start to panic and pick up my pace.

Another low flying light whizzes by my feet. Doing a skip-jump to avoid it, I almost lose my balance, scraping off half a cat's nose on one slipper. My fingers grip tighter on my doll case, and I take off. Darn those fireflies!

I make it to the next house, the Brimmers.

Stopping at their front porch steps, I blow out the remaining cool air from my lungs.

"Safe!" I gasp and shoot a victory smirk back to the street.

But something's not right here. What kind of disaster has hit the Brimmer's porch? There are huge piles of flattened cardboard boxes and crushed papers, all scattered everywhere. A green wooden plaque lays face down on a small table next to an overflowing ashtray. Light filters through wrinkled bed sheets hanging unevenly from the living room window.

As I walk to the door, my pillow catches the green sign's edge, spinning it off the table. Bouncing, it lands face-up on the door mat. It says: "Welcome to the Brimmers."

Aw, crapola! I forgot. The Brimmers moved away a couple of weeks ago. So, I'm standing on a creepy porch of strangers and about to ask them to take *me* in? Yeah, Vicky, great plan. Now, what do I do?

Scanning the porch, my eyes zigzag back and forth as if the answer is written across the air in front of me.

Wait. Hold your horses! Mom is our block's welcome-wagon lady. *I know—how's this even possible with her blues problem, right? But it's true.* So, this will mean she must have met them. So technically—they're not strangers. So technically—this one could be *the* one.

While I push a big ole empty swallow down my throat, I wonder, *Will I have better luck with a family I don't know? Or do I dare face the fact—a better chance with one who doesn't know me?*

A crack in my stubborn rock-hard armor is heard. And it was kind-a loud.

Must shake this off. And I mean—right now!

Setting my doll case down, I look around for empties—there'll be no more bottle catastrophes on my watch. I stretch on tippy-toes and push the doorbell. Nothing. I press a second, third, fourth time—well, it was more of a pound than a press. I'm obsessed with doorbell rings for some weird reason. And don't ask—I don't know what that says about me either.

No movements from inside. So, I knock hard right beneath the door's clear peephole. Within seconds, the tiny glass circle goes dark. Feeling sweat build beneath my palm, I grip firmer on the case's handle. And wait and watch. The peephole returns to clear, and off go the living room lights.

Wait! What? They're not gonna even step out to meet me?

My shoulders collapse. I hate all emotions; they hurt. It's like being pelleted with invisible bullets. And when I let feelings overflood my brain, it makes it nearly impossible to sort them out in my head. It's time to once again redirect the spotlight—tune out, detach, and move on.

This routine of mine—see how this skill comes in handy?

I spin around slowly, walk to the edge of the porch, and gaze at the dimming moon across the street. Its glow is being muted by a heavy fog rolling in right above the lined roofs. I watch as this cloudy blanket gradually lowers over my old house, my old yard, and my old family. Over everything.

Something starts to bubble inside me. My legs feel like wet sand is pouring into them. I shift my weight back on my heels and slowly spin around. With all these rejections, is there a *right* family for me out there? I'm not so sure anymore.

It's all becoming too much. Loud and long sighs spill out of me as I head toward home. My beat-up pillow and my bruised pride drag after me like dented cans behind a *Just Married* car.

Thankfully, being so filled with gloom leaves no room to worry about all the spooky evils surrounding me now. Or even the sidewalk cracks that I now ignore. For a second time tonight, I let my eyes leak. The drops glide down both cheeks as a weird sadness wraps around my thoughts. Can this be the same feeling mom struggles with every day?

No way—can't be. I'm too wrapped up in my chaos to make that kind of connection. *At least, not that I'd admit to yet.*

When I finally arrive home, I decide to hold onto what little spunk I have left and play down this final walk of defeat by taking long, proud strides across the porch. After many years of practice, my stubbornness refuses to give in to those bitter words from Mom: "Good luck finding your *right* family."

With my final defiant move of the night, I curl up on a wooden bench next to mom's array of half-dead potted plants. I lay my head down and use my pillowcase to wipe my last tear. My stubborn walls zoom up to surround my thoughts, and I close my eyes.

The robe's thick collar bunches under my chin, keeping me warm from the damp mist as I bury my head farther into the dirty pillow. Thanks to my heavy pajamas and warm slippers, I have a choice. I don't *have* to go back inside defeated. No—worse than defeated—wrong!

I roll onto my side. As one last pooled tear slides across the bridge of my nose, I pull the pillow in, squishing its softness harder against my face. With my hand extending outward from the bench palm up, my arm lowers slowly.

And just like that, my first tiny snore lets out, and I fall asleep.

CHAPTER 3

MERGE. TO. THE. RIGHT.

O ut of nowhere, a man's large, calloused hand clasps mine. With a tender pull, he encourages me to sit up, helps me to my feet, and guides me off the porch. While we walk toward the street, it's funny—I'm not scared. There's a comfortable sway to our connected hands, like the circus elephants do when holding each other, trunk to tail.

Elephants—I sure love them; can you tell?

My Gramp used to tell me an elephant joke. "How do you eat an entire elephant?" I would come up with many answers, but they were always wrong. "Someday, when the time is right, you'll know the answer."

But someday, never came. Ugh.

After a stretched-out yawn tugs on my eyelids, making the sides of my face sink in, I notice the man's right leg has a stiff catch, scraping lightly against the driveway.

"Gramp—is that you?"

He doesn't slow. His fingers pull on my hand, shortening the space between us. The moonlight sifts through thin holes in the mist and shimmers on his gray beard.

"Gramp? Gramp?" I say, again and again.

When we reach the sidewalk, he shifts his weight to face me and staggers.

"Merge. To. The. Right," he says.

"It is you! Where are we going?"

He struggles to lift his limp right arm, aiming his curled fingers outward. I look in the direction he points to, but it's hard to see anything through the thick haze.

"Merge. To. The. Right," he says again.

His heavy arm collapses back to his side, making him wobble. He catches his balance and continues down the sidewalk. Because he's pulling me, there's nothing I can do but follow. Only now, I'm the *one* holding tight to his warm hand.

A strange but familiar smell is floating in the air, something between ginger candy and sweet jasmine. Reminds me of an old perfume Mom used to have, called "Joy." Wonder why she's not wearing Joy anymore? *Of course I do—didn't take me long to answer myself there.*

We continue down the sidewalk when suddenly, poking out from the mist, a bouncing silhouette of a boat starts to emerge. Yes, an actual wooden boat. Parked like cars on the street, it's lined against the curb, tied to a mailbox by a rope of pulsating orange lights. As if bobbing on the water, the boat is floating on the most spectacular river of bubbles. Gazillions and gazillions of them. They're glowing in the most amazing colors you've ever seen. Each one is semi-transparent and coated with a slippery mixture of warping hues like soap bubbles have.

This shimmering river hugs the curb as it races down the street and disappears into the heavy fog. It's so unbelievable. This can't be real. Come on, this must be a prank. This was only a regular street when I walked past here.

I pull against Gramp's hold. With his light squeeze in return, he somehow tells me, "Everything is fine."

While he continues to tug me along, I twist my neck sideways to take a closer look at the glistening bubbles flowing by. As Gramp's pace picks up, my gaze comes off the amazing river as a second smaller silhouette begins to emerge. This one's inside the boat.

I barely get out, "Oh—wow," as the fuzzy shape shifts into a clear form, like zooming in on a blurry scene with binoculars. And there it is—a small old lady sitting on the boat's front bench.

Dressed simply, her top falls in wispy layers over baggy pants. All her clothes are the same color, a pale violet-gray; the same shade the clouds turn before a summer storm. She has an unhappy face with thin lips aiming downward. Her tired eyes are glazed red, like when you swim too long in a chlorinated pool. Her frown lines sag low, peaking under short gray bangs, with the rest of the hair tucked under a scarf loosely wrapped around her head.

Even without all the gloominess, she still looks old— real old. But with me, anyone over twenty is, well . . . old.

She stands up, spreads her arms out to steady the bobbing boat, and points to the wooden bench in front of her. As my heart begins to race, I pull back on Gramp's hand again. And like before, his gentle squeeze somehow whispers to me: "Relax, everything is all right."

I'm nowhere near convinced and refuse to take my eyes off her. I use Gramp's hand for balance, climb over the side rails onto the boat's curved floor, and sit on the middle bench. I'm more than happy to continue to give her the stink-eye.

"*Arumf*," she grunts as she plops down with a loud crash. The boat thunders as if it tried to talk back.

My heart is fluttering so strong that it's vibrating my chest. As all my thoughts go into overdrive, my head becomes full of swirling questions. I open my mouth to let the first one fly—but nothing escapes. For the first time in my life, I'm speechless. Great, now how's anyone going to believe this?

The Old Lady interrupts me coldly. "They don't have to."

Say what—? Did this old lady just answer my thoughts? My mind goes crazy. I stand with my mouth hanging wide open.

"Your Grandpa called for me," she says all hush-like as if it's some secret and she's trying to sneak me quietly away. "I'm told that you believe you're with the wrong family. Is it true?"

"Yes?" I say, just in case this one *is* a question.

"So, you think this is why you don't fit in," she says. This time—she's *not* asking. "Also, you think there's no one around you anymore who understands you." She squints her eyes down to a sliver. "And on top of all of this, you believe you're not getting enough love."

Oh boy—I don't like how all this sounds.

"Tonight, there might be a lot of things you don't like," she says. She blows out an impatient groan as if she's been yanked away from somewhere she'd much rather be. "So now that I'm here—you're all mine tonight. By morning, if you still believe you don't have enough of these things in your life, I'll be *more* than happy to send you to another family forever. This I promise you."

A promise? To me, that sounds more like a warning. And go with her? Tonight? I can't go anywhere with this old lady. How do I even know she'll keep her promise, anyway?

"Listen here, little girl," she says, her voice a low hiss. "If I say it's a promise, then you better believe it's a promise." She pivots her head from side to side as if shaming me.

My hands grip the cold and gritty wooden seat. I lean away from her, sliding my butt across the bench. *Rip,* a splinter catches my robe, tearing a small hole. My body stiffens as Gramp, whose hand is now patting my shoulder, gives me a nod. After I exhale an "I give up" kinda sigh, I lift myself enough to confirm the rip with my finger. It's a yes.

"Darn it all," I say as I flop back down. "Okay—okay," I grunt and begin one of my odd habits. Sometimes, when I must help my head sort things out, I rub my fingers over one another, kinda like washing your hands.

It's weird—I know.

My head hurts trying to figure this all out. *If only I could get a hold of Dad's Polaroid, someone might believe this. Then I'd believe this.*

"I said it already—this is *only* for you—nobody else has to believe," she says. The sadness in her old face reminds me of Mom's, only meaner—almost hateful.

The Old Lady gives Gramp a stern look. "You see, this is why I don't like to do kids—" she stops herself short as Gramp frowns and turns his face away.

"All right, I get it—only me," I say. *Geez—let's not blow a gasket, lady!*

Before my racing thoughts blast off to *crapola* levels, it's time for a few more rounds of my washing-hands routine. Maybe, if I calmly focus on the flowing river—instead of her sour mug—I can level myself closer to *cooler-ific.*

It's a miracle—my concentration is holding. A flood of buzzing excitement is replacing the pressure on my brain. "Boy, oh boy, this *is* magic—I told you!"

"No, this isn't—" she says.

"Yes, yes, it is!" I say, cutting the Old Lady off. "I know what this is! It's M-A-G-I-C magic!" Even after spelling it out—like a dork—I continue my unstoppable questions. "Is this where I make a big wish? I wish for—a new Barbie . . . no, wait, another ponytail . . . no, wait, a playhouse. That's it—my wish is for a playhouse!" Even with the Old Lady's piercing stare, I can't stop myself and almost choke on the speeding words that keep gushing from my mouth. "Am I right—am I? Is it *one* wish—is it *three?*"

The Old Lady's wrinkled face puckers up like a prune.

Might have used too much force there—better backtrack. "Please, and thank you?" I say, spreading on the charm.

We all stand motionless for what feels like forever. The Old Lady smirks and breaks the silence with a grunted laugh. And as unbelievable as it seems, I heard a small chuckle from Gramp.

"Stop—listen to me—it's not that kind of thing," she says, keeping her tense grin firmly in place. It's like smiling is something foreign to her.

But I don't care—not one bit. I can't be disappointed by a no if I'm barely listening to her. Besides, I'm getting a strange sensation that something wonderful is coming . . . and I don't get that feeling often.

Yes, even at ten, I know I'm different. I'll try to explain.

Take tonight. Most people—at least the lucky ones I know—have sharp imaginations. They can arrange their thoughts, picture them all laid out, then use humongous feelings to form ideas about where all of this is heading. *Heck—they could have even masterminded everything here tonight!*

But not me—know why? Because—to dream up what's happened tonight, you need a strong and organized imagination. So, if I can't hold my focus long and avoid feelings whenever possible, the ability to do this—is nearly impossible. It's as if I view the world like I'm watching a silent movie with bad actors I cannot understand or connect with. So, I follow the storyline frame by frame, unmoved. That's me.

When I visit my friend Mrs. C, she tells me not to worry so much. "Your imagination isn't gone; it's only misplaced. Give it time, and in your unique way, you'll find it."

"What about Mrs. Carol?" the Old Lady asks.

My throat goes numb. *Oh, my gosh! Is she answering my thoughts? She didn't—she couldn't?*

"Yes, I did, and yes, I can," she says without missing a beat.

I look to Gramp for reassurance—he's too busy settling into the boat's backbench to give any. He awkwardly maneuvers his bad leg and weak right arm, then begins fighting with the oars. He doesn't seem disturbed with all the crazy stuff happening around him tonight, so I guess I shouldn't either.

But how does the Old Lady know about Mrs. C?

"Because any memory you bring up, I can watch it along with you—"

"But you—"

"Yes, I can also hear your thoughts," she says.

Well, sure, of course you can. My hand flies up and cups my smiling mouth—nice to know I can still think sarcastically.

The Old Lady's eyes squint tight, then her attention moves over to Gramp. He's still battling with the two oars versus his one good arm. No sports announcer is needed to predict the winner of this match.

A puzzled look spreads across the Old Lady's face as if she's just now noticed he's disabled. With a slight smile, she gently touches her extended finger to the top side railing of the boat. A glowing beam shoots along from her point of touch to the back rudder.

"Burrum-rrrrr." A smooth sound of an engine turns over and purrs as a soft light illuminates around her hand, then lifts and disappears into thin air.

Gramp's eyes lock laser sharp on hers. His cold stare seems to scream, *"I can do it!"*

Oh, boy, do I know *that* look. For the record, I invented *that* look.

"With so much to do tonight, we should use the rudder option. Okay?" the Old Lady asks. It's the first time tonight she appears softer.

Gramp inhales a slow deep breath while his bottom lip wrinkles on one side. His frustrated face freezes in place—a true picture of stubbornness if ever I saw one.

Won't lie—I'm a bit tickled by it. *Is that how I look?*

Finally, casual-like, he secures the unneeded oars to their clips. Using his good hand, he gives a sharp flick on the glowing rope. It releases its hold from around the mailbox, springs back into the boat, and recoils like a snake next to his feet.

The Old Lady nods. The anger disappears from Gramp's eyes, and he lowers his head in return. He turns and grabs the handle of the humming rudder.

As we pull away from the curb, the Old Lady pivots to face the direction we are heading.

And off we go.

CHAPTER 4

RESERVED. PARKING.

The boat's bow slices through the river, churning up smaller bubbles from below. I spin in my seat to watch the passing streetlights bounce off the parting wake behind us. This is so cool—too cool to be real and way too cool to be happening to me.

"Let's get this over with," the Old Lady says. Giving me a hard look, she opens her hand palm down above my head, as they do at the carnival to see if you measure up for the big rides. Strange electric sparks begin to tingle and slither along my scalp, making the ends of my pigtails start to lift.

I flinch away. "Whoa, what are you doing?"

The Old Lady's hand jerks back, clenches into a fist and then is pressed against her hip.

"Listen here—you're the one who believes you're not where you're supposed to be. I have much better things to do than—" She paws at her shirt, then tugs on the top layer, not like the cloth is uncomfortable, more like a nervous habit. "Remember, this is *your* problem, not mine. So, if I were you—" The Old Lady clears her throat while squinting so tight that it's a miracle she can see at all. "Think about Mrs. Carol. Now."

With a stiff jerk, I sit up in my seat.

"All right. All right!" I say and raise my face toward the night sky. I'd rather talk to the man in the moon anyway. *Sure—it's easy for her to say, "Just think about Mrs. C." If that's what I must do—she better tell me how. Geez!*

"Really, again with the geez?" she says. She fires another glare as she grabs a loose end of her hair scarf and flicks it over her shoulder. "The only way—especially for someone like you—is to close your eyes. Got it? Now, must I say it again?"

I'll admit it's fun the way her witty sarcasm mimics mine, but if the Old Lady wants me to keep listening, she better think again. Especially after that *someone like you* comment.

Then *boom,* my eyes shut. Which is weird—normally I'm terrible at following directions.

Wait a minute; this proves I was right before—this *is* magic! My eyes fly open. I slap a hand over my mouth, covering my grin while my wide eyes bulge as if I'm about to barf.

After a long exhale, she does an eye roll—Old Lady style.

"As I said, concentrate on Mrs. Carol so we can watch together," she says. "It's like being in the front row at the movie theater. And the real beauty of it, thoughts have no vocabulary limits. It'll be like—" Her eyes narrow as she drags out a hiss under her breath. "Never mind, you'll see. Just do it."

My scattered thoughts with no limits—good luck with that, lady.

I press my eyelids tight as my thoughts shout at full volume. *Okay, I'm ready!* Apparently, I do nothing quietly.

"About time," she says.

Static electricity snakes its way through my hair once again. I flip one eyelid and catch her repositioning her hand above my head. I start to lean back, but that strange tingle pulls me toward her. She frowns, then gives me a slight nod.

Like I've mastered an ultra-cool skill, I smirk and close my eye. *Shut the front door—she's right; eyes closed is easier for someone like me.*

I like Mrs. Carol; it's Mrs. C to me. She lives across the street and is short and stocky—well, to be honest, she's fat like the mom in the Old Mother Hubbard book. And she's old, like way over forty-something years old—old. And she's, my friend.

Replaying my thoughts for the Old Lady makes me feel strange. There are details about Mrs. C I've never paid much attention to. From her floppy unkempt hair to her duster dresses in paisley dull browns, she's simply plain and unfussed. I'm not saying she's ratty or dirty, just different from our moms in their leftover 1950s dresses under starched aprons. And don't get me started on all their wasted hours spent on keeping every hair teased and sprayed in place.

"Get on with it!" the Old Lady says.

"My gosh—all right already!"

Mrs. C is a loner, making our neighbors think she's cold and hard around the edges. You'd never find her outside gardening or chatting with anyone from the Ladies Clubs. So, no big surprise that it's difficult for her to mingle smoothly at our block parties or holiday get-togethers. Then one day, she simply stopped coming.

Everyone says she's not a kid-friendly woman either. But, for me, that unfriendly lady didn't exist. Even after my annoying doorbell routine, she'll smile and give me a big bear hug every time I'd visit. And after, I'd always get a gentle pat on my back as she walked me down her front steps, watched me cross the street, and wouldn't move until I landed safely on my front lawn. For someone who disliked kids, let alone this skinny tomboy with a mule's attitude, she seemed to like me.

Not much good comes from Mom's "blues" problem, but her not caring where I go or who I see gives me the freedom to become friends with this sweet, odd lady. Go figure.

Many stories are buzzing the neighborhood about Mrs. C. One was about a meltdown she had when a kid cut through her yard after a ball and barreled into her mailbox. And another one is when Mrs. C threw a broom at a stray dog as it peed on the post of that same mailbox, then screamed while the dog ran away— along with her broom, of course.

Her other rumored notorious crimes were silly, like, "She's weird in a peculiar way," or "My cat's missing, and we smell Mrs. Carol cooking stew!"

Maybe every neighborhood has a Mrs. Carol, someone different enough from what is familiar, it stirs up an odd fear inside them. When neighbors refuse to understand each other, then on purpose look for a direction to throw this uncomfortable feeling onto, they do it. What better person than a sad, crazy lady who can't defend herself because no one was listening to her in the first place. Or a misfit girl like me, for that matter.

A faint ache is growing in the bottom of my stomach. "Am I doing it right?" I raise my eyelids just enough to see if she's still there. "I don't do things right, ya know."

"You're trying too hard. For Pete's sake—close them."

"Geez, okay, all right!" I say, letting my eyeballs do a half twirl.

On some visits, we'd sit at Mrs. C's kitchen table, roll up tin-foil sheets into cool crowns, and wear layers of candy necklaces. Mrs. C would laugh and rest her arms on her jiggling stomach as I waved Pixie Stix around like wands, pretending to be Glinda the Good Witch from The Wizard of Oz. *I would point the candy straw toward her face and say, "Are you a good witch or a bad witch?"*

Wait one minute—that's weird—I thought I have no imagination?

"Imagination always wants to be found," the Old Lady says. "Your Mrs. Carol, she sees it. Because you let her in, you're allowing her to understand you."

Wait one minute—I'm understood by someone after all? Oh, crapola! Forgot the Old Lady can see all this. My body slumps. I fling my eyes open right when she's pulling back her arm.

Ugh—it's too late. The Old Lady's barely used smile fits on her face better.

"Yes, of course—Mrs. C is one of yours," the Old Lady says. "That's how she senses things you need. Like finding your imagination."

"One of my what?"

Wait—I don't care—why'd I even ask? I must, must get a new family. I snap my look away from her, hoping to disconnect us. Must change whatever she's seeing, so I line up new thoughts: *No, you're wrong. You've got it all wrong. I'm N-O-T—not understood by anyone.*

I look straight at her and push a final thought: *Not even Mrs. C!*

The Old Lady lowers her eyes and looks away, shaking her head.

My tall protecting walls rise inside me as cold stubbornness floods my brain. I smile.

Yep—she almost got me there.

I look down at the glowing river as the waves smack against the front bow. Gramp uses the rudder like a boat engine and navigates us through the thick fog, zigzagging down street after street. The boat slows as Gramp aims us toward a familiar home where the mist hovers above an overgrown lawn.

He snatches the glowing rope with his good arm, swings it in circles above his head, then, with a snap, lassos around an old mailbox. Pulling tight on the rope, he secures the boat against the cement sidewalk. Gramp was raised in the big city—when did he learn how to lasso? Color me impressed.

"Reserved. Parking," Gramp says. His hand trembles as fingers point toward a weather-beaten mailbox. In peeling paint, the letters "C A" are barely readable on its dented sides.

"That box—I knew something seemed familiar. It's

Mrs. C's." We traveled all this way just to return right back to my street? That's so weird.

The Old Lady leans in, raises her hand above me, and nods.

Yeah—yeah, I can take a hint. I close my eyes.

Right after Mrs. C moved here two years ago, she replaced the standard Levitville box with this beat-up one. It went against the standard codes for the subdivision, but no one had the guts to make her change it back. What's even more strange is how Mrs. C won't use it, won't even open its door. I hear all her mail is held at the post office—and more bizarre—she even refuses to go down there to get it. How she gets her mail—who knows. This kinda unstable stuff gives the neighbors new excuses to misunderstand her. I always thought by the awful way the box looked that there couldn't be anything special about it. I'm not so sure anymore.

A heavy feeling squeezes my chest—the sad, serious kind of stuff.

I'd rather be distracted thinking about this super-cool magic than rewatch the sadder parts of my memories, anyway.

Oh yeah—it's so *that* time again. But as soon as I grab the spotlight and start to tune out, detach, and move on, the electric tingles over my head get stronger, pushing me out from this perfectly great distraction.

"For heaven's sake—get back on track."

"Okay, going—geez," I say and roll my eyes again. *Wonder how many eye rolls I can do in a day? Hmmm.*

At last summer's block party, I overheard Mrs. C's name. Two overly lipsticked moms were gossiping, their plates piled high with BBQ chicken and corn on the cob.

Back then, I didn't pay much attention from this moment on—but now, I'm being forced to watch the rest of their conversation.

"Mrs. Carol is getting crazier by the day," complains one. *"Went over to deliver her committee invitation; she wouldn't even open the door."*

"How rude," says the other. *They leaned into one another; you could tell they were just getting started.*

"I heard her husband was a local mailman from a small town, somewhere upstate. Mrs. Carol would leave his daily lunch in their mailbox, and then during his route, he'd stop and grab it." *The gossiping lady licked a dribble of sauce running down her pinky finger and leaned in closer. She used her hand to partially cover her lips as if she were passing along top secrets.* *"Well, I heard—one day he went to work, the lunch was never picked up, and no one ever saw him again. He died is my guess—left her battier than a fruit fly. Stay clear of her. And warn your kids about it as well."*

I jump out of the memory and reopen my eyes. The electric tingle in my hair stops. *Watching gossip up close like this—it's actually ugly.*

The Old Lady's harsh voice loosens up. "This is good—you feeling that? It's called empathy."

"Nope—I feel none of that," I say, almost yelling. If a drop of empathy is floating inside me, it must be denied. And fast.

Her voice goes deep and raspy. "No, huh? Guess we're going inside then."

The Old Lady's hand latches onto my arm, right above my elbow. Can't say I feel her grip; it's more like a magnetic bond connecting her to me. She begins rising from her bench. I'm lifted along with her. We float up and out of the boat, across the foggy lawn, directly for Mrs. C's front window.

"Watch out!" I scream, bracing for a crash. Then, don't ask me how; we glide through the closed window. Yes, through the glass. Just the way my favorite cartoon *Casper the Friendly Ghost* does it, melting into the glass then popping out the other side, whole again. "No way! Wait one minute! You *sure* I can't make a wish? How 'bout something smaller? Like, like how 'bout just *one* new Barbie?"

With the sneer I'm getting, the answer must still be a no. Darn it all.

The wonderful smell of brewing coffee fills the room as the Old Lady and I lower into the corner of the living room nearest the kitchen. We hover just above the floor. We can see Mrs. C at an old table eating her tiny dinner.

"Hi, Mrs. C!" I shout without even a thought. She continues eating her meal uninterrupted.

"Boy—you sure do blurt out a lot. You're one strange girl," Old Lady says. *Wait till she sees just how defective my thought-to-mouth filter really is.* The Old Lady turns and looks straight at me. "She can't hear you; this is from last night. Anyway, how did you know Mrs. C is a missus?"

"I didn't, well, not really." Words and thoughts fly between us, making it hard to tell where our *speaking* and *thinking* start and stop.

We are all taught since we were young that any older woman is a missus. So—is Mrs. Carol a missus? A widow? I don't know—don't think anyone ever bothered to understand the true story around her. Sad to admit, not even me.

It's true, I never did see a man during any of my visits, but I did notice on the end of the kitchen table sat an old photo of her standing next to a guy in a blue uniform. Their beaming smiles left no doubt that Mrs. C was happy then.

The Old Lady and I watch as Mrs. C finishes her dinner. Her hard-soled slippers clip-pity-clap on the kitchen linoleum as she washes her dish, pours a cup of coffee, and heads toward the living room. As Mrs. C takes in a long stare while passing the framed picture, her walk turns to slow motion. With a deep sigh, she pulls her coffee cup closer to her chest; her lips make odd shapes while they mouth silent words.

As if we're standing on an invisible conveyor belt, the Old Lady and I glide beside her. At this point, all I can come up with is, "Wow—oh wow." I might have said that out loud—again.

Mrs. C's gaze focuses on the old picture. Her heel catches on a small rug, which covers the edge trim at the beginning of the living room carpet. She lunges forward. Within a split second, the Old Lady touches the tip of her finger to the elbow of Mrs. C's coffee-holding arm. Just like on the boat, soft light illuminates from this point of contact. The glow radiates outward, then drifts upward through the ceiling. Mrs. C catches her balance.

If you ask me, a disaster was avoided, like how her cup tipped, spilled coffee over the brim, then swiftly caught by the saucer. I can't say the Old Lady magically prevented an accident from happening, but her fast reflexes seemed like a nice thing to do. Especially coming from her. I may not be the only person changing tonight.

"Whoa—how'd you do that?" I ask.

"I must try to do any kind thing, whether it does or doesn't change something that has to happen," she says with a muffled voice, then turns her face away. "Things I refused to do before."

"Before what?"

Within seconds, the Old Lady's small face contorts back to its original bitterness. With a twitch, she lifts one shoulder while lowering her chin toward it. Kinda like the way Mom pins the phone against her ear while using both hands to wash dishes. The Old Lady gives no more explanation while we watch Mrs. C plop down on an old couch across from her small TV that is already on.

The Old Lady points to the framed picture. Its position makes sense to me now. Placed at the precise angle, it's visible from where Mrs. C sits at every meal and from the faded sofa where she's now falling asleep while straining to watch the evening news. This precious picture must mean a lot to her.

I study Mrs. C's face, maybe for the first time. Her sleepy eyes softly hint at a quiet loneliness and sadness I had never noticed before. They look so sad; it makes me sad.

"It's because of empathy," the Old Lady says. "When you feel empathy for someone, it becomes a connection with them. You see, that's what understanding someone means."

Dang it all, I keep forgetting I can't hide my thoughts from her.

Nope—lady, you got me all wrong. Might as well fail me now. I won't go back to my old family. So there.

The Old Lady puckers her upper lip like she just smelled dog poo. She sneers at me, then points to a large book next to Mrs. C's steaming coffee on the table in front of her. Mrs. C gives a shy side-glance to an exposed sliver of paper that's been kept pressed into the book's crease. She pauses before pulling on the bottom of this small note with tenderness and tremendous fear at the same time.

"We must read what's in that letter," the Old Lady says as she leans in for a better view. I also move closer.

Gladys,

There's nothing I need to say to you anymore. Sandy and I are together now, and we'll be living far away from here. I won't be coming back, ever. There's nothing I want from you, not even a divorce. Deed to house is in your name, so sell it, don't sell it, I don't care. Do whatever you want, say whatever you want. Just say that I died. You'll never hear from me again and I don't ever want to be found.

Walt

My mouth goes dry. A pressure climbs up my throat and tries to escape through my eyes. As we watch Mrs. C cry softly, my heart feels like it's being squeezed from within. Mrs. C's pain seems so real—feels way *too* real—to me.

"No wonder she's misunderstood," I say, as the pressure builds inside me. "Didn't even know her name is Gladys, let alone all of this about the mailbox. And that story about her husband dying—not true at all. He left her. That's even sadder."

"Now you get it; now you're understanding," the Old Lady says. "With the sorrow that came after being abandoned, she couldn't accept her situation; it affected her very being. Her mind is unable to regain a stable footing. So, instead of moving on, she holds to her reality as best she can. She uses their old mailbox as a beacon, hoping patiently in her grief that someday he'll find his way back to her."

Right, lady! *Her very being, hoping patiently in her grief?* You went way too deep for me there.

The Old Lady squints to hold back a sparkling tear. But it's too late. It pools under her eye, drops out and curves upward, so it never hits the ground. And like before on the boat, a soft glow radiates around the tear as it floats up through the ceiling.

Even with my tough stubbornness, I know something good and meaningful just happened. Hard to believe none of the neighbors bothered to learn any of this. Tornado thoughts spin inside my head—time to take my deep breath and start my counting routine. Ten, nine, eight, seven . . .

There's a strange feeling inside me, like clearing out space for something new, something more. Is it empathy? And, with everything Mrs. C's going through, how's it possible for her to understand me? And, why me? Is it my endless girl chatter, my entertaining Glinda wand waves, or maybe she's just happy to have someone sit in her kitchen chair? The one not used by a family that no longer visits.

So, let me get this straight, even with Mrs. C being misunderstood by everyone—until now, that included me—she sees my lost imagination and helps me find it? With tonight's rewatching, it's becoming clear to me: Mrs. C understands what it's like to be misunderstood.

"Allowing Mrs. C to understand you helps you to understand her," the Old Lady says with a smile. She places both hands on her hips in a proud stand, like the huge jolly man in the Green Giant commercial. "Yes. You've learned empathy."

Not falling for any of this again, I'll fight her every step of the way. I do my proud stance. "So, bottom line: I failed, right? Let's go meet my new family."

The Old Lady gives me a disgusted look like I have cooties. Her face twists as if she swallowed a lemon.

Back-at-cha, lady.

The room goes still and cold. Like mirror images, we look away from one another. Mrs. C's cries cut through the air in the room. We return our gaze full circle, back onto Mrs. C's weeping sweet face.

The phone rings and punches through the silence. We both flinch, breaking our trance from Mrs. C's pain.

I start to speak, but the Old Lady brings one finger to her lips. "Shhh," she hisses. Yep, she's sure getting to know me.

Mrs. C raises her head, wipes her soggy eyes, and slowly walks to the kitchen. As she lifts the phone's receiver, her chin dimples and quivers slightly.

"Does she always look this upset when she answers the phone?"

The Old Lady nods. "Yes, she's petrified. Always preparing for bad news about her vanished husband."

Mrs. C's glossed-over eyes grow big. Her trembling hand presses the receiver to her ear while she allows her sad gaze to escape through the kitchen window. Her lips slowly part as her bottom lip trembles. "Hello?"

The Old Lady does her pressure grip on my arm. We both float up, move away, and head back through the window.

Something's happening. I've got this strange sensation tugging on me. Somehow, it's making me want to stay and hold Mrs. C's tiny hand. This type of tenderness is unusual for me—but there it is. As we float over the lawn toward the boat where Gramp is waiting, these new emotions build inside me. With a quick snap of the rope, the mailbox is released. Gramp steers us out and we race fast away.

Jagged icebergs are melting inside my chest. I withdraw my eyes, along with my heart, and in silence, we leave yesterday behind.

CHAPTER 5

BUS. PARKING. ONLY.

S tirring up deeper layers of bubbles from below, the river's roar is now angrier as it tosses a stronger ginger-jasmine scent into the air.

We sway and bob with erratic jerks as we zoom down the street. The Old Lady grips tighter to the boat's side rails.

"Hang on," she says. "Things will be getting a lot wilder from here on."

Our speed increases. Clutching the rudder firm with his better arm, Gramp fights to point the bow toward a small wooden home. His knuckles turn pale as he struggles to maneuver the boat. It's becoming too difficult to control the boat's aim and we slam into the curb's edge. With a hard *thud*, we ping-pong back into the bubbling river. Gramp wastes no time and with a one-arm throw, he lassos their mailbox. He yanks on the rope until the boat's wooden side scrapes against the cement. I uncurl my fingers, releasing their grip from the side rails and look out at the mist as a home peeks-through the fog.

"Where are we?" I ask.

"Bus. Parking. Only," Gramp says. It's surprisingly clear over the loud sounds of the splashing waves. It's a challenge understanding Gramp with his road sign words—but this time, his words aren't making any sense.

"Gramp—this isn't school," I say.

Old Lady answers what Gramp cannot. "He knows that—he's not dumb, you know?"

"Yeah—I know!" *I'm far from dumb myself, lady.*

One side of my lip twitches. It's a true miracle my attention span is still holding on. I get that she's mad this night isn't going her way, but I'm right in the middle of an important mission here. If I can keep ignoring her bitterness—hold my focus a bit longer—I'll be in a brand-new family by morning. Dealing with this cranky old lady should be easy for me. Let's face it, I know my way around unhappy people—look at my family.

"Are you listening to me? You really don't pay attention—" Old Lady cuts herself short while yanking on another layer of her blouse as she did earlier. Only this time, with a noticeable tick. Her mouth twists and turns like she's silently counting while flattening a curled-up edge on the material.

Well, that seems familiar—is she copying me? Can it be that when she gets mad, she becomes super nervous? Or do I make her feel like this? *If so, better get in line, lady— you're not the first person to react this way to me.*

With a tight squint, she scans me over, then points toward a small home. "This house belongs to your bus driver."

Beyond the mist, I see a variety of home styles sitting on lots of different sizes—some big, some small. This means we can't be in our evenly plotted Levitville any longer.

Thanks (not!) to another one of Kiffer's info dumps, a distraction takes over again: "Ford's assembly-line-built identical homes … blah, blah, completed every sixteen minutes … blahhh …"

Good grief—why do I remember this junk?

I switch off the Kiffer lecture and try my hardest to refocus. "Oh—you mean *my* school bus driver, Mrs. Dryver?" *Mrs. Dryver's real name with matching job name—you must admit, it's way hil-lar-ious.*

A half smile takes over my lips. The Old Lady sighs, and her foot starts tapping on the boat's wood floorboards as she places her hand above my head.

"Okay. I'm going, I'm going." The moment my eyes close, she jumps into my thoughts.

I was almost six when I met Mrs. Dryver. I was finally allowed to go to the Big School as if there was a Small School comparison. Didn't bother me if Smarty-Pants Kiffer started a year earlier or slow-to-mature me started one year late; it was my first day of real school and I was super excited.

The bus pulls up. With lights flashing all around me, I do a quick inventory: class supplies—check, one metal lunch box—check, one doll—oh, crapola! With no time to run back home, the surrounding air begins to push in on me. Then with a loud wham, these large glass doors banged open, and there sits Mrs. Dryver. This unbelievable control center is spread out in front of her with cool knobs, levers, and blinking buttons. I stand there, mesmerized.

"Hello there," Mrs. Dryver says, peering down from her high command post. "I'm Mrs. Dryver, and who are you?" I remember feeling a warm wave pass through me, like when you gulp down hot cocoa on a cold winter morning. Somehow, my thoughts smooth out. What Barbie?

A sudden feeling of dread presses on my chest and shoves me away from this good memory. "Oh no!" I snap my eyes open. "Does this mean I'll have to think about what happened on the bus today? Nope and double nope. Don't want to."

"It'll be fine. Come on, close 'em so we can watch it together."

The muscles underneath my frown throb as I try to stall, but nothing comes to mind to de-fleck her curiosity from today's awful bus incident.

The Old Lady gives me a shooting glare. "Well?"

"Fine, fine! Hope you know what you're in for," I say. My heart races. I squeeze my eyes tight, inhale a deep breath, and brace for the worst.

Immediately there are arms, legs, and screaming grunts as white liquid flies everywhere.

I instantly tense up and pop open my eyes. I tried telling her—people never listen to me!

Startled, the Old Lady's arm springs back to her side. "Wow, um—wow. Okay—" She re-extends her arm. "Close 'em once more—I'll take us past all that—we'll watch from a safer distance."

As my eyes close, we pop inside the memory, past the fight and why it all happened in the first place. And the memory begins again.

The Old Lady and I hover inches above the wet lawn outside my house. I watch the falling spits of rain slide clean through us. They hit evenly on the ground beneath our feet.

How cool—she's right! It is like watching a movie—only the views are somehow expanding. We can see both inside and outside the house at the same time. It's like nothing blocks us from watching anything and everything attached to the original memory. And think about it—this can't be just from my memory anymore; at this point, I wasn't even here yet. My Elvis smirk happily returns.

We watch Kiffer leap out of the school bus onto the curb and walk down the sidewalk. A drizzle taps on the rim of his Yankees hat as he moves with a pack of boys until one by one, they trail off toward their homes. Of course, Kiffer doesn't even notice or care that he's walking home—without me. Yep, I might as well be invisible.

We can see Mom in the kitchen opening a bottle of Pepsi Cola, quickly trudging back to the living room where the TV is on. She passes the front window and peers out at the school bus turning at the end of the block. Mom's face shows no emotion as she scurries back to her soap opera. She seems unaware that only one of her two kids returned home from school today. Does she care? I don't know.

Kiffer walks across the wet lawn past where the Old Lady and I still hover. Stopping before our porch steps, he looks down the street and sees his buddies getting greeted with hugs and kisses by touchy-feely moms surrounded by cigarette clouds.

The only thing we have in common with them is the cigarette clouds. We are not those kids. And for the first time, I notice Kiffer realizes it as well.

Kiffer may have seen enough. With a slight frown, he does what looks like a long deliberate blink, then turns his head from those doting kid-mom reunions. Is this his way to tune out, detach, and move on? Or do these mushy types of feelings never fully penetrate him in the first place? Let's face it; it could just be another one of his odd quirks.

Either way, a sudden frenzied smile bursts across Kiffer's face. He bangs the front door open. Throwing his stack of books and lunch box onto the bottom step of the shag carpeted stairs, he rushes toward the kitchen. Kiffer's whole face looks like it's about to explode as he yells back toward Mom.

"Mom—guess what!"

Mom looks up, not focusing on him but simply to acknowledge what she heard. With a dismissing nod and a shush wave of her arm, she darts her eyes back to her show, which, by the sound of overly suspenseful organ music, must be building up to a big ol' cliffhanger.

Kiffer's not bothered by Mom's reaction and continues to shout from the kitchen, "Need two dollars for a field trip. We're going to the Museum of Natural History next week!"

He pours a glass of milk, grabs a napkin with some oatmeal cookies from an old ceramic jar on the counter, and then heads back to the stairs. He stops right before the edge of the living room carpet. Knowing no food is allowed outside the kitchen, he dunks each cookie with a precise soaking time that only he knows, then shovels them into his mouth. One by one, they all disappear.

"Mom. Need two dollars!" Kiffer says. With a louder force— and his mouth full of cookies—he sprays wet cookie bits every- where. Kiffer snaps his hand to his mouth to block the rest of the shooting crumbs. He sees some juice spilled onto his books from

his turned-over lunchbox. He quickly takes the napkin, steps the forbidden two steps onto the carpet, and smears the drops off. With a quick peek Mom's way, his panic look melts. He swipes the lunchbox and heads back into the kitchen while gulping down the last of his milk. After dropping his lunchbox and glass into the sink, he walks back to the stairs and grabs his books.

"Mom!" His face strains to keep his eyes from rolling to the back of his head.

Mom looks up as her soap opera goes to commercial. There's Kiffer, standing with his books tucked under his armpit, posed like a runner waiting for the starting gun.

"What? I heard you!"

"Ugh, " Kiffer says and dashes up the stairs.

Within seconds, he runs back down, less his Yankees cap and books. He carries a large tub of molding clay and a plastic table-cloth to cover the top of the kitchen table. As Kiffer dumps the tub out, it makes an embarrassing noise as it releases some trapped air that's held the clay to the container's bottom. It resembles—well, let's just say, a bathroom potty problem. After the big gray blob plops on the table in front of him, Kiffer plunges his hands in. His face relaxes as he gets lost in his daily routine, constructing his clay town monstrosity.

Love that word monstrosity, don't you?

Not sure how Kiffer can so easily go into such a deep zone. His eerie concentration is amazing and annoying at the same time. Even with us being the same age, he can focus on one thing in complete silence for hours, days even. And be happy about it. Unlike me—and my five-second attention span—I'd rather chatter and fidget, lose total interest, then just flit away.

Why am I so different?

Mom sits, holding another lit cigarette while she gazes an unfocused stare at the laundry commercial. It's an overly loving mother watching her young daughter smell a teddy bear that bounced into a basket of fluffy blankets.

Yeah—like Mom and I can relate to that whole scene.

She takes a big gulp of the soda. Her puzzled face darts around the room. With a "something's not right" look, she tilts her head, raising an ear upward as her chapped lips take another drag. The only noises in the house are those awful potty sounds from Kiffer's clay.

Mom takes a few more pulls of her cigarette before putting it out on the bottom of a vomit-green glass ashtray. "Where's your sister?" she asks. It's a miracle. I can't believe Mom noticed. Maybe it was the laundry commercial? Yeah, not hardly.

"Don't know," Kiffer says, using his favorite standard answer. Lowering his voice, he uses it again. "Don't know."

"What do you mean—you 'don't know'?"

"I don't know—" His lips push out so far it distorts his face. "Think she had another fight today; Mrs. Dryver made her sit up front." Kiffer pulls his shoulders back, all proud-like. He rolls his eyes like loose marbles, drives his hand deeper into the clay blob, and rips off another big chunk. I know my brother well enough; he thinks it's not his job as the golden child to look after a dumb sister. Yeah, good job there, Kiff!

"That girl! What's she done now?" Mom's eyes open wide, and her jaw drops as if she meant to say that part only to herself.

With the TV still on a commercial break, she snatches her soda bottle and walks over to the living room window. Pulling the shear curtains to one side, she watches the last straggling kid disappear into their house. She knows it's common for me to be yakking away and completely miss our driveway. Within minutes, I should realize it, then head back home.

Mom squints at her watch, smirks, and presses her powdered nose against the metal blinds. Her frown is so tense it pulls her ears in slightly. Looks like my lateness may disrupt her unfinished soap opera.

Mom walks back to the sofa and lets out an angry sigh. "Go over to the Garafolas—see if she's over there. Tell her, home right now."

Kiffer is knee-deep into his clay building zone but emerges enough to grunt. "Aw, come on, Mom. Do I have to? You know she'll be—" He stops playing with the clay and leans his chair back to get a better view of Mom's angry face.

She shoots him that look—we all know that look when we see it.

"Oh, man!" Kiffer's entire mouth balls up into a knot as he stomps toward the front door. From this angle, I never knew my brother could look so hilarious. Sure hope the Old Lady is watching this—she can use some humor in her life.

Kiffer opens the door as our school bus parks in front of our house.

"Mom, Icky's home!" Leaving the door wide open, he spins around and bolts toward the kitchen, back to his clay town.

Mrs. Dryver and I walk off the bus. I'm wiping a splatter of Elmer's glue off my nose as she fights with an umbrella while putting her arm around me. My dress is a disaster, pigtails every which way, and my new black Mary Janes are scuffed up with deep white marks. Mrs. Dryver gently squeezes my shoulder while making a few more tweaks to my appearance: straightening my collar and pushing back dangling stretch ties, barely propping up my sticky pigtailed hair. It's use-less—I'm a complete mess.

Mom's eyes stay fixed on the TV as she slowly makes her way to the open front door. "How many times have I told you, young lady? Straight home from the bus!"

Mrs. Dryver leans down and gently rubs my shoulder. With a sweet smile, she whispers, "Don't worry, Vicky. I'll explain every-thing." Mrs. Dryver struggles to straighten her body; her gait has a funny wobble as she walks beside me. She must have the same fat problem as Mrs. Dorsey.

By the way she tries to cover me under the umbrella—or, at least from our angle—it's clear Mrs. Dryver cares for me. Like, a lot. It's even clearer as I lean away from her, forcing my opposite shoulder into the light rain—I want no part of it.

We make it to our porch steps as Mom arrives in the doorway. "Vicky, what have I told—" she peels her view from the TV just in time to see I'm not alone. Her face stiffens as she presses out a forced grimace of a smile. "I mean—missy, where have you been?" she says, turning light red in the face.

"Sorry, couldn't let Vicky come home in this condition with-out explaining," Mrs. Dryver says, her voice trembling slightly. "Had to drop the last kids off first. You see, Vicky fought with a kid—a bully, I should say. But don't worry; it was all over before I stopped the bus. Thanks to your daughter here—there'll be no more problems with that boy ever again."

Mrs. Dryver makes it sound like I knocked the kid off—or at least knocked him out. I kinda like both versions.

While the Old Lady and I watch, I'm embarrassed by how uninterested Mom is as she stretches her neck for a quick view of her show. Mrs. Dryver notices as well. She gently pats my back, kneels, and spreads her arms out wide. Still feeling lava pumping through my veins, I turn away from her. My stubbornness is fully intact.

It confused me when this fight had happened, like being out on a thin limb with no tree attached. My thoughts piled on top of each other. Feeling like a hero for what I stood up for on the bus. But also, mad—who's standing up for me? No wonder it left no room for me to notice Mrs. Dryver surrounding me with her love.

With one hand on her belly, Mrs. Dryver struggles to stand up, then softly taps the top of my head and scoots me toward Mom. "I'll see you on Monday, Vicky." I merely grunt and walk past Mom into the house.

"Thanks for explaining; you're right. I would have wondered," Mom says with one eye and ear still straining its attention toward her now resumed show. Mrs. Dryver turns and waddles back to the bus as Mom closes the door.

Refusing to come down from my adrenaline high, I slam my battered books on the stairs and huff my way into the kitchen. I shove a stepstool against the cabinet to grab my three cookies. My blood is boiling. So mad, I stuff all the cookies in my mouth at once and chomp. I don't even care about drinking any milk.

Kiffer does not react to this; he's too engulfed in his clay town to care where I've been or what happened at the door. After a few dry cookie coughs, I yank a chair out and flop down. I reach to grab a piece of clay.

Kiffer freezes, mumbling, "Don't think so." He pulls his attention back into his clay construction zone. Without warning—even to me—my tongue shoots straight out, stuck full of gooey crumbs. Kiffer must remember from the last time I played with his clay.

Clay got crammed in the wheels of his matchbox cars and it took him forever to get it all out. Nope—can't say I blame him here.

Mom looks happy to be back to her show and her cigarettes. The Old Lady and I watch Mrs. Dryver step back into the bus. She groans as she squeezes into her seat, then drives the bus away.

Great! Rewatching the memory has gotten me all fired up. My shoulders get so tense that they're almost touching my ears. I flip open my eyes to see the Old Lady's arm fly back to her side. I, Gramp, and the Old Lady sit motionless in the bobbing boat still docked in front of Mrs. Dryver's home.

"I'm not gonna watch any more of this," I say and spin around toward Gramp, away from the Old Lady. "See, I'm not loved—Mom didn't even care." My words cut through the silence. "I'm ready for my new family now."

Reaching over, Gramp taps the top of my clenched hand, then gives it a soft squeeze. Slowly, my fingers relax.

Oh boy, the Old Lady's eyes turn into slivers—boy, does she look unhappy.

"Okay—guess we're going inside then," she says.

She does that energy grip on the back of my arm, and like before, we float out of the boat, across the lawn, then through the front window. Lowering gently in the living room, we see Mrs. Dryver on the phone. She sits near a small kitchen table set for two. Things are heard boiling on the stove while the most wonderful smell of bread floats in the air. The warm feeling that's building inside me gets pierced by Mrs. Dryver's begging voice.

"Mom, please talk to me," she cries into the receiver. "I miss you—I need you."

As Mrs. Dryver pauses to catch her breath, we hear the distinctive *click* from the other side of the line. Mrs. Dryver weeps as she places the receiver on its cradle. Looking toward her stomach, she caresses her huge jumping belly. Seeing her without her coat on, I'm surprised at how fat she is.

"She's not fat, silly—she's going to have a baby," the Old Lady says.

"A baby? Not-uh—that's just fat," I say like it's a known fact. The Old Lady seems too amused to argue.

We watch as a man, I'm guessing her husband, takes his hat off while coming through the front door. His dark eyes go almost flat as he smiles. He looks different from all the rest of our fathers. His skin is very tanned, and his straight dark hair is so black that it reflects a blueish shimmer like the feathers on a black crow. If Kiffer were here, he'd explain: a crow's plumage, iridescent, light ... blah, blah, blah ..."

I've never known anyone who looks like this man before—especially here in Levitville. Is he Chinese, Japanese? Oh, crap, could he be from that war place—the one that's been on the evening news a bunch lately? Viet—Vietnam?

I take a half step back. The Old Lady's bonded grip yanks on my arm. "Where are you going?"

My throat goes dry. "Nowhere. Um, I'm watching—I'm watching!"

Wearing his concern over a warm smile, the man walks over and wraps his arms snugly around Mrs. Dryver. She buries her face into his chest, her shoulders relax, and her sorrow seems to drain away. After kissing the tip of her nose, he uses both hands to steady her fat belly. Bending down, he tenderly whispers something to it.

Even I can tell they're in love. So much that it's spilling over. I've never seen love like this before—not really. I won't lie—I kinda like it. A warm feeling melts something cold inside of me.

Looky here, Old Lady; you could learn a thing or two.

I get a sharp glare with a quick smirk from her in return. "Hmmm. Yes, this one—it's most definitely the one for love. You barely let Ms. Dryver love you; you don't let your mom give you any—guess you have your reasons for that." The Old Lady's words seem tense and crack as they come out. "The simplest of these is the one for love. It can also be the hardest one to let in."

"One of what?"

The Old Lady's lips tighten. "Fillers, of course—one of your connecting gap fillers." Her words sound bitter, as if I should have already known this.

Like preparing for a long, boring speech, she wheezes in a long, deep breath. "Every one of us fills gaps. Well, at least we're supposed to. There are millions of different gaps with as many different types of gap fillers trying to help.

Fillers of gaps? Yep, she already lost me. I pop her another *say what* kinda face.

"Okay, look at me," she says. She scans me over. There's a calmness to her now, making her almost likable. "We're all intertwined. It keeps us connected—meshing one person's strength to another person's weakness." She then continues in the most boring voice, like she's reading an instruction manual. "If someone is not being loved enough, let's say by their mother—" *Yeah, subtle as a freight train, lady,* "they feel vulnerable and unprotected. Small gaps develop. These holes need fillers to close the space. If too many of these filler moments are unsuccessful, the gap deepens. If they grow too big, our minds will find ways to protect us and build tall walls around these holes, brick by brick. And if the walls are allowed to rise too high, you can get blocked in, permanently."

I look at my stomach then stretch to inspect my backside. Nope, no holes that I can see.

"You can't see them, silly girl," she says, whipping her eyes to the sky. "Listen, no one's life is perfect—but most of us do fine if we simply allow the fillers to do their job. But on occasions, a gap gets created so big and so deep that a different kind of filler is needed. Let's just call it universal justice, karma, God—whatever you want. Your Mrs. Dryver, right here—she's a special kind of one. She's the one for *love.* Everything gets filtered through this special love kind, so it's often the first to clog up."

Is she calling me a clogger-upper? After rewatching myself tonight, I'll admit I might be stopping *some* of my filler moments. Don't think I do it on purpose; I just don't want to let anyone—or anyone's pesky feelings—come too close and overwhelm me. Is that so bad?

Would some of this information help explain Mom?

As weird as it sounds, something inside me feels fuller. It's not coming from my gazillions of quirky thoughts and rambling questions that constantly bunch up—it's closer to that satisfying fullness you get after a big bowl of ice cream.

The Old Lady's lips loosen into a tiny smile as a sparkle grows in her eye.

"It's time for us to go," she says and reaches for my arm.

CHAPTER 6

SECURITY. ON. DUTY.

Like before, the Old Lady's magnetic grip clamps down on my arm. We both rise and push out of Mrs. Dryver's window. Slicing through the thick fog, we reach Gramp, whose face has tightened and gone serious. That sweet smell of jasmine and the river's power have increased. By a lot.

As we stop above the wooden seats, Gramp fights to steady the boat from the strong force of the current. The boat's sideboards scrape against the cement curb. It drowns out the *umf* that slips out of the Old Lady's heavy sigh as she plops on the front bench.

After only a moment to settle, Gramp gives a swift snap of his wrist and releases the lassoed rope from the mailbox. With a roar, we zoom away and watch Mrs. Dryver's home fade back into the mist.

Turning in my seat, I study Gramp.

The moonlight bounces off the water and reflects onto his tired face. It reveals a twinkle of joy in his blue eyes as if tiny light beams of percolated happiness have penetrated the back of brilliant gems. Smiling has been impossible for him since his stroke, but there's a lift to his face that resembles one. He sits straighter, prouder, even taller from when we began tonight's adventure. With the help of that powerful rudder, Gramp must feel great having free control over his mobility again.

Tell you what's not great—it's never noticing he has blue eyes—until now. Okay, I'm not the best granddaughter—but I'm trying to be a better one. At least I can say I'm thankful he's here with me tonight; there's no way I could have handled all this without him.

My heart feels lighter, and my mind less noisy. Honestly, it would be super cool to believe that when a filler moment is successful, it can help fill the holes our complicated lives create. Well, that's if you believe that filler moments are real in the first place.

"We should give and gain something from our life's journey," the Old Lady says, interrupting my thoughts. "This is what each day is supposed to bring us. That's if we let it."

I allow her words sit inside my head for as long as my focus can hold them—which, unfortunately, isn't long.

The boat takes a sharp turn at an intersection. Then slows. As we pull up to a creepy home, any glimmer of joy left on Gramp's face has disappeared. He wrangles his lasso around another mailbox and ties us off. Then he carefully steps out to support the Old Lady as she exits the thrashing boat.

As she grips his arm, I wonder who is supporting whom here. Does Gramp feel her touch, or is it only the bonding force I feel? And what's up with that anyway?

You'd think the Old Lady must have heard my mind's questions, but this time, her motionless face isn't showing any answers. She seems preoccupied, almost hypnotized with Gramp.

Eww—I'll bet it's one of those grown-up things. Yuck-o!

After the Old Lady's feet land on the sidewalk, she steadies herself, releasing her grip from him.

Next, it's my turn. Holding tightly on Gramp, I time my exit jump with the bobbing of the boat and leap over the railing onto the damp sidewalk. Tada!

"Where are we?" I ask.

"Security. On. Duty," Gramp says. A sadness sits over his blank stare.

I—for sure—do not like this house.

Its worn shutters are barely hanging on by broken hinges, and their front light's glass is broken, exposing the bright bulb to a family of suicidal moths. It's not just because of the night that makes this small house seem dark and eerie. It *is* dark and eerie.

"Whose house is this?" I'm afraid to ask, but I do. The Old Lady looks at the ground as if she's lost something. She walks around to the opposite side of the mailbox.

Please, don't tell me she doesn't know where we are either.

The Old Lady looks at me, then over to the mailbox. I can see on the box's metal side that the name Shilaski is scratched through with the name Bennett written over it.

"I know that name; it's Shilaski," I say, sounding proud as if I've solved a hard riddle.

"Ralph Shilaski?"

"Yes, that's him," I say. "He carried me home today. After my accident."

"Accident? That must have been scary."

"It was, and he is. Well, maybe he is," I say as the scary stories kids blab about him start flooding my brain.

The Old Lady shoots me a snarky look. The same one I give when hearing we're having stew for dinner. "Not *that* stuff," she says. "Now, think—the moment just before the accident. It happened after your mom called you both in for dinner—directly after, right?"

"Yeah, so." The way she asked bugs me for some reason. Why did she need to know an *exact* time anyway?

Her forehead wrinkles. "Don't be a smart Alec. I need a specific place to start from—that's why. You know the drill—let's get this over with."

Sarcasm—it's sorta been *my* thing. But hearing hers return—as if it ever left—felt somehow nice. My scalp begins to tingle again. And off we go.

Our block has an extra security layer living two doors down. If there's any problem in the neighborhood, we know who to call—our very own ex-Marine cop, Ralph Shilaski. Around here, we kids have a secret theory—this policeman is really Superman. When the evening news broadcasts the evils from around the world, Mr. Clark Kent here, somehow keeps all the bad stuff outside our block. It makes no difference if he works all night and sleeps all day—knowing the big man in blue is within yelling range makes us feel safe. I believe in his super-duper power so much that I go speechless whenever he's near me. You'd think this huge cop has two heads or something.

"Enough of that—come on!" the Old Lady says. "Focus. Closer to the accident."

"Okay, geez."

We watch Kiffer and I ride on one bike together. He peddles while I steady myself on the thin fender holding tight to the post beneath the bike's seat. With a goofy smile plastered across my face, my skinny legs flop from side to side on each of his pedal strokes. We ride the sidewalk down to Mr. Shilaski's driveway. Then, turning into the street, we head back toward our house and return to the exact point we started.

Sometimes, Kiffer has repetitive quirks—but nope, I'm not complaining—because today, the boy that rarely wants to play with me is letting me ride along.

Mom yells from our kitchen window. "Come inside; dinner!" Hearing the pitch in her voice—and the fact that she's even calling us for dinner—says Mom's having a good day.

Like before, this memory view comes alive. It shifts and changes, making it possible to see inside and outside Mr. Shilaski's dimly lit home all at the same time. The Old Lady must be maneuvering everything here. But how? This is my memory; she wasn't even there when this happened. To see everything around a memory, I don't care what she says; that's magic, all right.

"Pay attention," she says, cutting in with a snort.

Still surprised at how real all this looks, I reach up to touch my face, making sure my lids are closed. They are.

Like a close-up in a movie scene, our view zooms into Mr. Shilaski's house. Even though it's dinnertime, there's no food cooking or signs of his family anywhere.

Mr. Shilaski's head bobs as he slouches on the sofa, his shifting legs rub on makeshift bedding. With puffy skin under half-open eyes, he's listening to our biking outside.

Is this what he does during the day, exhausted, yet he still tries to watch over us?

We see stacks of long white papers full of sad words, like D I V O R C E. Beside them lay empty food wrappers and an over-flowing ashtray. Ugh—those smelly cigarettes—the way everyone loves to smoke, you'd think they must taste like chocolate. Adults, they make no sense at all, if you ask me.

We can also see Mr. Shilaski's gun resting strangely on his chest. The Old Lady goes silent; she isn't even attempting to explain what's happening here. It feels like I'm being pushed to figure out what this is. Even if what they say about me is true—that I'm slow to mature or behind emotionally—it's plain to see. Mr. Shilaski's sad and alone. Is he contemplating that thing no one thinks about—at least, not out loud?

Can this be like that thing with Mom from a few years ago that no one would explain to me? That never-spoken event that may or may not have happened. From what I remember, it was a weird time in our family. Yes, weirder than usual. Mom had disappeared. Strangers babysat us—late night whispers of Dad on the phone downstairs, neighbors talking in hushed tones while delivering cas-serole dishes tagged with scotch-taped instructions. It holds a space in my memory like shadows hiding in the corner of a dark room.

I refuse to remember any more of this. I want out of this memory. Now.

Suddenly, the crashing of metal is heard along with my unmis-takable screams. In one swift motion, we watch Mr. Shilaski jump up, slide the gun into his shoulder holster under his jacket, and bolt toward the door. Did his original intentions get deactivated?

As the Old Lady and I hover, our views trail directly behind him as he barrels out the front door. Stopping at the end of his driveway, he pauses to inspect this mess sprawled before him. With mind-blowing shrieks that only a kid like me can master, there I am, all laid-out, interlaced in the bike with my entire foot sandwiched between the spokes.

Mr. Shilaski looks calm like this trauma is just a routine day for him. Leaning down, his strong arms gently wrap around my waist. He lifts me, along with the connected wreckage, and lugs this entire ball of chaos across our lawn.

Watching it all happen from this new angle, I study our neighborhood's hero up close. What felt like forever at the time only took a matter of seconds for him to easily transport this pile of intertwined metal, arms, legs, and blood-curdling wails in front of my pale-faced mom waiting at our front door. I remember feeling surprised my arms didn't want to release from around his neck. His face inches from mine forces me to see he's not as scary as I had imagined—or as bad as the kids built him up to be. Looking at his chiseled jaw and bushy sideburns, I don't feel the same scary way about him anymore. I must see him for what he truly is—a regular man wearing Superman's muscles.

When this all happened, I was so wrapped up in my catastrophe that it never crossed my mind to think about Kiffer. Now I watch as he nervously scurries behind Mr. Shilaski like a mama dog trailing someone who's carried off one of her precious pups.

I get it, Kiffer—a bike is what's important; a sister, not so much.

Couldn't remember how I got detangled from the wreckage. Now, I can watch what my original memory didn't record: Mom's body is jerking with small tremors as her shaking hands untie my grimy shoelace, slip my tennis shoe off, and support my bent foot. Mr. Shilaski simply pries the spokes apart using his superhuman power—and like that, my foot is free.

Then, without a sound, this great hero of a man stands up. He plods down the street and unceremoniously vanishes through his front doorway into the darkness.

"Wow, the power! Just—wow," is all I can say.

To have the feeling of being protected is unusual for me, especially after experiencing such pain wrapped in bike metal. But I can see right here I am. Does Mr. Shilaski know the difference he makes in the neighborhood? As for me, I now know he owns a cape and Clark Kent glasses.

Yep—he makes me feel safe. Maybe I do trust someone after all.

The Old Lady's face molds into a relaxed smirk. "The real key to feeling protected and safe is to let yourself trust and depend on someone."

"Crapola!" A burning wave travels across my face. Darn shared thoughts. Old Lady must have me mixed up with someone else—cause this girl is getting a new family. I may not be the best at staying focused—but tonight—this is how I'm gonna play it: To win, I must plan to fail. I slam my defiant brakes on my thoughts and fling my eyes open.

The Old Lady's eyebrows rise while she retracts her hand back. "So, little girl, you're telling me you don't see this extra protection?"

"Protection? No," I say as quickly as possible. "He just wanted me—and my screams—off his property so he could sleep. That's all that's about."

The Old Lady's face molds back to its harder form, which is a shame; she was starting to look friendlier. She turns toward Gramp, whose lips have tightened flat.

"Okay, guess we're going inside then," the Old Lady says and latches on my arm.

I'm pulled over a half-dead lawn then through the window. Her hard grip pinches my skin under her tight hold. Either she's getting stronger, or the magnetic pull is more powerful. Even if it's a fantastic way of entering homes, I can tell—this is no time for excitement.

We land in a gloomy kitchen. Like in a hospital waiting room—bracing for bad news, we watch a man and woman sit silently at a kitchen table. Their blank expressions stare at the extra place setting in front of an empty chair.

"This is Ralph Shilaski's home—when he was a boy," the Old Lady says. "See the man over there—it's little Ralph's new stepdad, Mark."

The back door flings open, banging into a pair of muddy work boots sitting on a newspaper. A boy about my age runs into the kitchen, yanking off his jacket while pulling on his dirty sleeves to cover greenish bruises on his arms.

Yuck—his arms.

"Shhh—just listen and watch," says the Old Lady.

"Why the hell are you late?" Mark screams. "Go back out. That seems to be more important to you."

"We just sat down—it's fine," little Ralph's mom says. She springs up and grabs the empty plate, her feet tripping over one another as she hurries to the stove.

"Hell, it's not—why must you baby him? When I was his age, if I were late for dinner, I'd have no dinner at all."

For a moment, as if daring little Ralph's mom to react, he keeps an intense stare fixed on her, then returns his scowl to the boy. "Go upstairs so we can eat in peace. Now."

"Mark, no—it's okay. Here, I'll put a little on his plate—he'll eat quickly, then go upstairs—you won't hear another sound from him, I promise."

Little Ralph hesitates, slowly lowering his jacket on the back of the chair, and sits down. Mark slams the table hard with the palm of his big hand. No doubt, to make the sound louder. The vibration makes the mom and boy jump, each sliding their chair back. Seems to be a scene they've experienced before.

"Please—Mark, let him eat?"

Little Ralph stops between sitting and standing, so much so you can't tell which way he's planning to go. Then it's decided. In a calm motion he leans forward to sit.

Mark springs up, grabs little Ralph's thin upper arms, and slams him toward the floor. To brace his face from the impact, the boy struggles to free an arm from Mark's firm hold, but Mark keeps the grip tight long enough to make that impossible.

With a terrible *thud,* little Ralph hits the kitchen floor, face first.

As she holds back the volume, fear cracks her tiny voice. "Mark! Why did you do that?"

"Only pushed him toward the floor—not my fault he's uncoordinated. You got one clumsy kid there."

Little Ralph covers his face with one hand while pushing himself up with the other. A little blood oozes out between his fingers.

The Old Lady's face loses its hardness. She moves closer. Using a finger, she attempts to touch the boy's trembling arm. Her entire hand passes through him. Even though this didn't seem to help little Ralph, a small glow builds, encircles her hand, then drifts upward until it fades into the ceiling.

The Old Lady lowers her head as a sad moan slides between her lips. Her eyes and mine do the same thing— they fill up. Without touching the Old Lady's cheek, a glowing tear falls, then recurves upward, never reaching the ground. Like the glow, the tear radiates light, heads up toward the ceiling, then vanishes into thin air. *Why didn't her touch help? And what are those glowing lights, anyway?*

Little Ralph walks slowly out of the kitchen as his mom weeps into her napkin. Mark sits back down, grabs his fork, and stabs into his dinner.

I'll be honest; I don't have it this bad at home. But wow—even with all the bullies at school—I've never seen this type of meanness. My bully meter explodes. I'm not sure if I should scream or jump over the table and punch Mark in the nose.

"Your magic—why didn't it help?" I say like it's all the Old Lady's fault.

She presses her lips with the tips of her fingers and looks away.

"It only works if it doesn't change something that must happen later. Kind deeds, even ones that won't make a difference, should always be tried. See that glow? That's the *energy,* the *love* it produces. That's what counts—that's what adds up."

"Adds up? I don't understand."

"Think of it this way," the Old Lady says. "Imagine you have a goal. And this goal is to fill a glass. Each kind filler moment you attempt—successful or not—represents a drop of water. If you ignore and reject your filler moments, the glass won't get filled. And you lose." She adjusts her scarf into a collar so thick it hides half her face and muffles the rest of her words. "I lived a long life, wasting many of my filler moments—ignoring many times to be one and rejecting others who tried to be mine. So for me, it'll take a very long time to catch up." Her magnetic grip pulls on my arm. "It's time for us to go," she says.

"No, we have to stay!" I yell and tug against her bond. "We can't leave—no one's helping him. Where are *his* fillers?" The more I fight, the more her grip burns. Rage grows inside my gut—I'm gonna be sick to my stomach. My face scrunches up on one side. Can I convince myself this Old Lady knows what she's talking about?

No way—there's no way. I'm not convinced.

"Oh, don't you worry; little Ralph will be getting a protection filler soon," the Old Lady says like a whispered threat. As she leans in—too close for my comfort—her wrinkled lips gap open. "Listen up—there are many things I'm not supposed to tell you. This guy Mark, he's going to refuse an important filler moment. Let's just say, after next week he won't be hurting anyone—at least not physically—ever again."

"He's gonna die?" I ask, sorta hoping.

"Nope, but he'll wish he had," she says. "Mark is what can happen when *all* filler moments are rejected—none being accepted, and for sure, none going back out. It doesn't matter if you believe it; everyone has the power to be a filler. Filling—and getting filled by each other—is how it all works."

Confused as usual, my dazed stare should be enough proof I'm not grasping this connecting-gap-filling-kindness junkola.

"It figures—kids like you need a picture painted for them. This is another reason I don't do kids." She sounds just as irked at having to explain it more than I am at listening to it. "All right let's give it another try. Imagine you're in a hot air balloon, floating over an ocean filled with man-eating sharks. And let's say the goal is to travel across, hopping from one safe island to another. Picture your *fillers* as the balloon's air blower and the actual *filler moments* are the wind. It's all up to each of us. You ignore either of these two things, and chances are, you'll end up drenched. And with many nasty bite marks to boot. Get the picture now, little girl?"

Really? She's plum crazy if she thinks after saying "kids like you" that I would pay attention to her anymore. It's true—I've not been the best student tonight—but let's be real here, I only asked for a new family—not a new teacher. Teachers, I've got plenty of those.

The Old Lady's eyeballs glaze over. Her mouth has this tight smirk to it. "All right—I never liked that analogy anyway." The Old Lady moves in closer. She looks over her shoulder as if someone is trying to eavesdrop on us. "Listen up. Soon his hand will be painfully crushed at work—beyond saving, in fact. One afternoon, his physical abuse will end abruptly. And remember those hungry sharks? They'll be getting a nice big feast. You happy now?"

Yes. Awful as it sounds—there is satisfaction in knowing all this. But I'm not a patient kid. So, her idea of "soon" isn't soon enough! Even if she's been right on a lot of things tonight, my bully meter wants satisfaction. Today. Now.

"I'm not leaving him—not like this." I pull hard against her grip. By how she yanks me back across the lawn, I'm quickly reminded I'm not calling the shots here.

The Old Lady and I lower onto the boat. Gramp's knuckles have gone white as he holds the rope tight. It's a miracle the boat didn't get swept down the now ferocious river.

Gramp seems upset. I can tell how his closed lips flatten while he moves his jaw up and down, like he's chewing gum. Bet he knows the awful things we just saw inside.

"Security. On. Duty," he says. Gramp's loud voice is stronger. The Old Lady's eyes soften as she looks toward him.

The boat is bouncing a good foot up and down now, creating smaller and smaller bubbles. The way the agitated waves crash into the sidewalk reminds me of how the Old Lady's lessons are smashing against my stubbornness.

Again, my thoughts zoom back to little Ralph. My insides rage at the unfairness of it all. Just when I was ready to agree with her, I feel something boiling over, blinding me. He needs help now—I don't care what she says.

"Girl, can't you hear? I told you—it will be over soon. You want to know *why* all of this has happened—isn't that right?" I'll never understand—why can't anyone ask me a question as a question? *See, it's not so hard if I can do it! Ugh.*

As the rage builds inside me, I'm not sure what I want now. I think I'd rather stay furious at everybody than learn any stupid understanding-kindness crapola.

"*This* is what happens when anger takes over," the Old Lady says. "Understanding, kindness, and love—poof—disappear." She raises one eyebrow high like Jack Benny does in the middle of a joke. "What remains is hate, bitterness, and misunderstanding. Sometimes certain things must happen and play themselves out. They can't be stepped over as you do with those cracks in the sidewalk. It may feel unfair, but there are times the created kindnesses that follow outweigh the bad."

The Old Lady's thin, wrinkled lips curl into a tiny smile. She locks eyes with Gramp as if they have a silent way of talking. After a shallow sigh, she turns back to me.

"There are a million reasons why filler moments are delayed or rejected. But most of the time, they sit patiently in front of us. It's a shame how often our choice is to simply ignore them—you know—the way you do with Mrs. Dryver? Some filler moments get ignored for years or even a lifetime. Trust me here—*this* I know all too well."

Trust. I'm trying—but there's too much fire burning in my thoughts to listen—let alone trust her. With these strong feelings brewing inside of me to do something to help little Ralph, I can't leave him, not now.

No, make that I *won't* leave him.

Can't this lady see it's a waste of her time? I may not get physically hurt like little Ralph is, but I still understand what it's like to feel alone. And sometimes not protected.

So, if my lesson is to learn empathy, fail me now because that feeling is long gone. I want to fight.

"Okay—listen." The Old Lady's sharp words cut into my thoughts. "Mr. Shilaski's terrible experiences were bad, no doubt. But they also made him better at protecting others. Like with your bike episode, he has a strong need to watch over you—along with all the kids around here. Try to look at filler moments as chains that connect us. Ignoring or rejecting even one is like breaking a link. It severs the love energy from being produced or passed on. When you trusted Mr. Shilaski's help, it showed you haven't shut him out and didn't block his filler moment."

If I admit I get enough extra protection by these filler moments, then I'd have to rethink . . . well, everything.

I need a minute here to calm my insides. I twist in my seat and look out into the mist. This is so confusing. To me, it sounds like collecting points.

"Collecting points; that's an interesting way to think of it," she says, giving me a puzzled look. "You're a protective filler yourself—did you know that? That's why you go after bullies."

It's true; I've always hated how bullies prey on anyone different from themselves. When I see one—especially in action—my head heats up, destroying all normal reasoning. Like this energy building in me right now—it's shoving me to do something. Vicky, do something!

"Now, hang on there before you get out of control." The Old Lady's tense eyes study me from head to toe. She exhales a sigh that sounded more like a low moan. "I can prove what I mean. Go back to today's bus fight—this time, from the beginning."

The beginning—the real reason for the fight? All she needs to know is it was all because of a dumb bully. Okay, it's also because of the odd way my brother stays inside himself. But not the same way Mom does—it's more like his concentration is so intense that everything around him disappears.

Because of this, it makes him such an easy target. Sometimes even by me.

But I didn't do anything to Kiffer today—not today— and I wasn't gonna allow anyone else to either.

CHAPTER 7

SPEED. BUMP. AHEAD.

"Speed. Bump. Ahead," Gramp says, surprising us both by adding his two cents. How clever of him; even though it's been a long night, Gramp is still on it. Nice.

As the boat fights with the river's turbulence, it pulls on the rope, making the lassoed mailbox vibrate. The way the Old Lady nestles into her seat tells me we're not going anywhere anytime soon.

"Now, girl—start just before the actual fighting begins," she says, almost demanding.

She's wearing my trademark look of stubbornness on her face, so it's probably useless to challenge her right now. Besides, I want to get passed all this stuff and see my new family.

So, I shut my eyes. It's still amazing; it really is like watching a movie. When it starts, our view this time is from a high ceiling angle inside our school bus.

The bus is packed full of kids. There I am, sitting two rows behind Kiffer. He's so deep in his dinosaur book that a bomb could go off and he wouldn't notice.

"Kiffer loves dinosaurs; he wants to be a paleontologist someday—"

"Shush—not now," she says, putting her finger up to her lips. "Concentrate."

"Good grief, I was just—oh, ugh."

Seated directly in back of Kiffer is the school's meanest bully, Chuck. He snickers behind my brother, ready to perform to this bus's stupid audience—at Kiffer's expense, of course. I can always detect a bully a mile away. I possess my own bully meter; it's a special power of mine—you know—like a sixth sense. I'm the bull part of a bully—fighter for justness—a fairness equalizer—

"Enough already. Move on," the Old Lady barks. The tingle in my hair gets stronger.

"All right—I was just—geez."

Chuck raises a large bottle of Elmer's glue over Kiffer's head, preparing to give him a glue shampooing. Today, the bully thinks he's found his prey: my brother.

Too bad, so sad, Chuck! The school's best bully buster sits right behind you, and her eyes are laser-beamed on the back of your dumb head. Crushing all bullies is my rule. Age difference, or even my scrawny arms, won't matter at all. Any normal kid would never get involved—but I'm far from normal. My official record for the year: Vicky 5, bullies 0.

One of my favorite techniques for dealing with bullies is to stay outside their radar until it's too late. And for me—too late is when my bully meter turns on, activates my feet, and I'm storming in. Most of the time, this full-on blinding attack works. If the initial pounce doesn't do the trick, I've been known to bite cheeks and shoulders and push my fingers up their noses—basically, do whatever it takes.

"Stop it. Stop leaving the memory to speed talk in your head," she says. "You're getting me so—"

"All right, all right!" I told her I didn't want to re-watch this—but as usual, no one listens to me.

We continue to watch me—the bully buster—jump over the back of Chuck's seat, reach from behind, and latch tight around his neck like a squid grabbing its dinner. I must say, I look pretty darn strong, my whole fifty-five pounds and all. That's soaking wet, mind you.

Chuck frantically tries pulling me off. I'm so close and tight that he can't punch, push, or kick me. While I keep a firm grip on his neck for leverage and clinginess, his eyes look wild as I yank his hair and pull on his ears.

Even as I rewatch this, I can't tell which of these two entangled kids are making all the loud grunts, moans, and shrieking screams. When the timing feels right to disengage, I spring off and push far enough away to stay out of reach. Landing in the aisle, I'm positioned like another attack is imminent—in case he's stupid enough to want more.

Rewatching all the anger that's oozing from my vicious eyes, I can't help but smile. At the time, I thought the fight lasted much longer. Now, I see it was over as quickly as it started.

Chuck is disoriented as if he can't remember his initial plan. He smears white glue from his sleeve onto his jeans.

"You're a psycho," he yells and sits down cool-like as if planning on doing that all along. As if! My theory: bullies are only

scaredy-cats. They aren't evil enough to beat the power of my awesome assassin energy.

"Enough of that—stay on track," the Old Lady says as the tingle beneath my pigtails increases.

Mrs. Dryver jerks the bus over, then fights with her belt while doing belly maneuvers to get out of her seat. She waddles down the aisle toward us as I quickly reclaim my spot on the bench. I didn't realize how bad I looked. My pigtails are every which way, socks and dress are cattywampus. Blobs of Elmer's glue drip from my nose and down the sides of my cheeks. "Looking like something the cat dragged in," as Gramp used to say. Yep, I miss that Gramp so much.

Mrs. Dryver steps past Chuck's row to mine. Her face softens as she pats my shoulder with such tenderness. With a light touch to my chin, Mrs. Dryver lifts my head and smiles, then steps one row forward and stops within inches of Chuck's right arm. She begins to tap the front of her shoe on the floor.

With a blob of glue dangling from his ear, the coward Chuck looks ahead like he's not a part of any of this. Then, without a single word, her cheeks flush pink and the shoe tapping stops. The entire bus goes silent. There'll be no squealers here, thanks again to more unspoken kid codes.

It's fascinating, all these details. I didn't notice them before. Like that panic on Chuck's face and how he slowly diverts his eyes away from Mrs. Dryver as if there's a huge spider staged on his shoulder. The way she's planted in the aisle—it's obvious she's not moving till he looks back at her. Chuck blows a heavy sigh, then looks up.

"I'm gonna bust you so badly if I ever see this again," she says, so faint it was frightening. No one had ever seen Mrs. Dryver look at anyone like this before. Heck, no one has ever seen her look angry before.

So busted! Chuck turns and looks out the window; it's all over. He's just been schooled by the scrawniest girl and the town's sweetest bus driver. The bully has become humiliated.

Mrs. Dryver returns another look my way, smiles sweetly, and walks toward the front of the bus. Grunting as she plops into the driver's seat, she looks through the large rearview mirror, reaches back, and taps the empty seat behind her. I know what this means. I grab my stuff and walk the winner's aisle past Kiffer, who had barely noticed there even was a fight—let alone it was supposed to be his. I can just hear him now: "There goes my dumb sister, in trouble again. What a dweeb."

While the rest of the bus watches silently, I sit behind Mrs. Dryver. As we pull out, the loud bus noises suddenly resume and flood the air.

As far as I'm concerned, I've shown the Old Lady enough. When I reopen my eyes, she's looking straight at me. My denial is ready, positioned nicely at the tip of my tongue. Come on, lady; ask me again so I can shout, "No, no, no." If *she* fails tonight—then *I* fail tonight. This means I win—new family, here I come.

With the bully fight replayed and finished, adrenaline pumps through my veins. It's building up angry questions. As usual, I'm confused. Why, after protecting someone else, does it make my insides scream, my palms sweat, and an alone, sad feeling takes me over? Maybe there's gonna be more to learn tonight—hopefully more about myself.

With a slow deep breath, the Old Lady pulls her hand back and brings it to her side. "When *people*—no, let me change that—when *I* was young, I stayed trapped in my selfish head. Rarely did I listen to any of those deep nudges telling me to do kind things, even the smallest ones. Now, I'm forced to gather all those moments I ignored before."

"Before what?" I ask.

"My before. Listen—it's important you learn this—close your eyes, so you won't miss a thing."

Closing my eyes is now becoming an instant reflex for me—all I do is think *eyes closed,* and *ba-bam*—they close. Having my body react to my commands with little effort feels pretty darn awesome.

Without missing a beat, the Old Lady speaks into my thoughts. *The heart always nudges us toward filler moments. The specific kindnesses we do for others determine what kind of fillers we are. Remember also, ignoring these filler moments, they won't go away. Both the hole and its nudge grow.*

As if her thought words used up all her air, she takes a long breath and continues. *When I was young—younger than you—my heart was silenced. It created a gap so big that I shut down inside. This allowed tall walls to build until one day I was trapped. From then on, any tickle of a nudge became a nagging burn. Finally, it became a form of sickness in me.*

Her sad thoughts have quiet pauses between the words. I sneak a peek at her closed eyes. There's a warm glow surrounding her softened face. It radiates outward, evaporating in all directions. While I still fight it, important portions of what she's saying may sink in.

"I don't expect you to grasp all of this," she says. "You've been through a lot tonight and shown more than is normally allowed. In time, you'll forget a lot, but the good stuff—the *really* good stuff—will stick." She tips her head at Gramp and then turns to me; her voice feels direct, final, and sad. "Goodbye, little one. Remember what you can—remember me—I will always remember you."

"Wait—what? The night can't be over yet!" Waves of terror race through me. "No! No, I can't leave yet—I'm not ready." I'm not so sure of everything anymore. "I was—I was wrong." I force my words out so hard that the air stings my throat.

As if she didn't hear a thing, the Old Lady turns sideways in her seat and looks out at the sparkling river.

"Goodbye, Grace," Gramp says softly.

My stress turns into shock. "What?" I look frantically toward the mailbox. "No! Please, Gramp—tell her—I don't want to leave!" But Gramp is no longer there. The rope he was holding dropped and now lays flat on the ground.

"Gramp! Tell her I want to stay—don't let her send me away!" I jerk back toward the Old Lady named Grace—but the boat's benches are empty. She is gone as well. I spin in my seat and stare back at the rope on the ground. "Oh no, I was wrong. I understand. Gramp, please, tell her I understand!"

More panic floods me. I'm alone on this bouncing boat, surrounded by misty fog. I spring to my feet. The boat wobbles. I lose my balance and flop down hard against the seat. As the boat starts to pull away, the dragging rope slithers along the ground until it slides off the curb and submerges into the raging river. I feel something grab the front of the boat, yanking it hard away from the curb's shoreline.

Looking down for something to hold on to, I grab the bench tight on either side of my legs and hang on for dear life. The loud, angry bubble waves are several feet high now.

My grip keeps slipping as the boat leaps off the top of each wave. It hits midway into the next, only to swing up its slope and leap across to the following one. For a split second, my mind escapes to the beginning of this night, when my biggest problem was wearing inside-out pajamas. *Oh—if only that were true now!*

The boat roars along. Its wood frame bends against the wave's pounding hits, making awful noises. Frothy bubbles fly up the boat's sides, jump off the railings, and slap into my face. The strong winds lift the larger ones higher; they pelt my body then deflect off to be left behind in the dark mist. That sweet smell of ginger-jasmine is so strong that it's becoming unbearable.

I hear the rudder break away. *This must be the end; I'm doomed!* The peaks of the waves smooth out while the boat accelerates. I watch the trees, mailboxes, and parked cars go by so fast that I can barely tell one from the other. Only white flashes now—the light poles buzz as they whizz past. When I think I can't take one more second of this, my eyes slam shut—and with everything I have, I let out one long final scream.

CHAPTER 8

RESUME. SAFE. SPEED.

At the end of my long blood-curdling scream, everything goes silent. Has it been a few seconds, minutes? Or, because I may no longer be alive, does time even matter anymore?

There's an empty feeling of nothingness around me—no movement, no sound. I slap my hands against my face to cover my eyes that refuse to reopen. Is this a normal reaction? *Heck, right now, I don't really care what's normal.*

Everything is so black. I can't say for sure if my eyes beneath my fingers are open or closed. And I have no desire to find out. My entire body is now frozen in place—except for my breathing, which has become a heavy pant like our neighbor's collie does in the summer's heat. Nope, not going to move one single inch.

With every heartbeat, the veins inside my eyes pulsate so strongly that I feel them against my sweaty palms. I can tell—even in total darkness—there's a weird feeling of movement. Not like the wind blowing your hair or clothes, more of a strange weightless pressure. It's an unusual sensation, as if everything around the boat is moving at a high velocity. Yep, I said velocity. It's one of Kiffer's favorite words. *Of course, Kiffer has no problem pronouncing the V in velocity!*

As if this will make everything disappear, I press my fingers against my eyes so tight, my knuckles go numb. Not sure—am I more disturbed by this strange form of travel or petrified where I'm being taken? Pretending not to learn a single thing tonight from the Old Lady—I mean, really, what *was* I thinking? Boy, did I make a lot of miscalculations tonight. Darn stubbornness—I've really failed now. And now, it's too late.

Gradually, the speeding forces around me slow. I rise straight up as if gravity has left Earth and I'm being lifted into space. My body tilts horizontally like an upside-down plane coming in for a landing. Then, as if laid flat on a billowing cloud, a gentle softness touches my backside.

Sooner or later, I'll have to find out where I am. So, I release a courageous hand off one closed eye and reach back. My fingers paw at a cloth material and I twist my fingers around the fabric, tightening my grip. Is it the same on both sides? Only one way to find out. I remove my other hand away from its squinting closed eye. Okay, it's the same on both sides.

A paralyzing wave of fear floods in. If I'm still alive, I could be anywhere—but where is anywhere? And, if I am alive—have I now been sent to a *new* family? What kind of home will it be, what kind of mom and dad will I now be stuck with? And a brother—will I even have a brother? Or a Mrs. Dryver, Mrs. C, or a Mr. Shilaski? These thoughts never crossed my mind during my entire quest. I may never see *any* of them again. There's an ache throbbing in the middle of my forehead. And my Gramp! Gosh, he may no longer exist in my new life. Crapola, now I've *really* done it!

The only way to find out where I am is to open my eyelids and look. Keeping my grip tight on the fabric behind me, I brace for the worst and slowly open my eyes. And I mean *slowly*.

My focus comes in gradually.

The room is dark. I look toward my feet and wiggle my toes hidden under a soft blanket—*my* Kimba blanket? Raising it enough to peek under, I stare at faded pajamas with inside-out cats. But this proves nothing—I can still be anywhere. Then, there it is—my beat-up Barbie case sitting on a dresser with my thick robe slung over an opened drawer.

I can barely make out the window across the room. Tiny beams of light slip out between the curtains. As usual I'm too excited to think. I toss off the blanket and sit straight up. My forehead smashes into the wooden planks above, and I ricochet back into the bed. I'm such a numb-skull—that's what I am. And that's what I painfully got—a *numb skull*.

With my head spinning from the impact, I lean over the side and scan the floor, making sure there *is* a floor. Then, tucking my head, I roll out. Landing with a thump, my bare toes curl and grip the soft shag vomit-green carpeting.

So far, so good!

I race to the window and throw open the curtains, almost yanking them off their rod. The light cuts in and reflects off the falling dust, filling the room with microscopic snowflakes. I lean into the glass—if I see Mr. Shilaski's house, then I must be back home.

And there it is, the *big man in blue's* home—which by the way, *is* painted blue.

"Yes! His driveway—it's empty!" I say so loud you'd think I found the cure to cancer or something. But typical curious me, I need more proof. I run to the dresser and snatch the robe to check the back for a fresh hole. Yes, and yes! At least I know I haven't lost my mind.

The smell of toast hangs in the air.

"Kiffer, I don't care if your cream of wheat ran into your eggs—eat it!" Mom's voice barks out. More typical breakfast voices rise up the stairs from the kitchen. *My family's* breakfast voices. I'm home—I'm home!

Throwing the robe down, I open the drawer wider and grab a corduroy jumper with a pullover sweater. I peel off my inside-out PJs, which now turns them *right* side out. *You've gotta admit—that's pretty funny!*

I run down the stairs while fastening my last corduroy strap. With a final leap, I bypass the last two steps and land squarely in front of the kitchen entrance. *Wow, that's a first for me!*

The sight of my brainiac brother, Gramp, and even my indifferent mom, sends a jolt of excitement through me, warming my entire body.

I know—I'm surprised at this also.

Kiffer's devastation is plastered all over his face as he stares at the food disaster on his plate. For a split second, I feel bad for him—until I don't. I've got more important things to worry about and way too much to tell them.

Where do I start? Hundreds of thoughts flash through my head with such explosive energy that it jams my brain.

I lunge straight for them, overshoot, and hit the table's top. My hands yank on the tablecloth—but Mom's one step ahead. She holds firm, pressing palms down, and grips the edges of the fabric. Everything on the table stays in perfect place. I stand back up, fully recovered, as if we've rehearsed this near catastrophe a thousand times. And maybe we have.

As I begin shouting all the details of last night's amazing adventure, Mom simply releases her grip, and with zero emotions and buries her face back into her newspaper.

"You won't believe this! Last night—it was so, so cool! Gramp took me to the street, put me on a boat with an Old Lady—"

"Yeah, right. You're such a fibber," Kiffer says. "I should sell your friends tickets to hear all this make-believe stuff. Oh, that's right—you don't have any."

This is probably the closest thing to my brother saying a joke—I'm impressed, really. But instead of telling him so, I decide he deserves something better than a compliment. So, I scrunch my face and flash him with a fat smile and a fatter wet tongue. He returns my look with one of his own, then views the unfathomable mess in front of him once again. His shoulders droop and he lets out a defeated sigh.

"Gramp was there—he'll back me up," I say. "Remember Gramp? *Security on duty? Bus parking only?*" Gramp sits unfazed in his *stroke zone,* looking outside, far, far away. "Come on, Gramp! How about *merge to the right?* Anything?"

A burning sensation hits my face, making the skin on my cheeks feel prickly. What's happening here? They must believe me; this is important stuff. "Listen to me—there was this mist and glistening bubbles racing down the street—and this old lady, she—"

Mom's hand flies up to halt my rambling. She pours cereal into a bowl, throws milk on it, and tosses in a spoon. Plopping the bowl in front of me, milk splashes out onto the table. She then returns to her breakfast.

I stare at Mom. I mean, really look closely. I hate to admit I haven't paid much attention to her for a long time, if ever. Maybe there is something in common between us. What if the challenges we both struggle with are some of the same things? Like, our lack of imagination? If it's true, I can't blame her—you can't teach something you don't have.

Can her mood problems create my mood problems, or can my mood problems create hers? Maybe, it's as simple as she has her reasons for being different, and I have mine.

"That's enough," Mom says. "It was just a dream." She takes a long pull on her cigarette, then puts it out by dragging it in circles in its ashes. "Last night on the porch, you were out cold within minutes. Had to disturb your dad just to get you upstairs."

Then she points toward her lap. "Yes, I was on the phone, watching you from right here the entire time." She smirks as if proud of herself, then looks through the kitchen window, far, far out, at a sad something way in the distance. Something none of us can see but her.

It takes me a second to absorb everything she just said. "No—that's not true!"

Mom wakes from her semi-trance and shoots me daggers. I now have her attention—but not in the way I wanted.

"It's *very* true. Each neighbor was told to just say no. I made sure you'd have to come back home—and don't give me *that* look—you're the lucky one. *My* mom—she would've locked the front door and left me outside to sleep in the cold. All night." Her raspy voice lowers. "Plus—she'd been happy to do it too. And with a name like Grace—what a joke."

Mom looks startled by the abrupt information that just escaped from her mouth. She slams the paper shut and jolts to her feet. Practically throwing her dishes in the sink, she rushes out of the kitchen.

She may not mean to hurt me, but perhaps she realizes she does. Nope. By how her mouth is hanging, the only thing she realizes is she said too much.

While I sit stunned with this new information, Kiffer swirls large pieces of scrambled eggs and pushes them away from his runny, hot cereal. He leans his head back as he watches Mom walk out of sight. He puts on his stupid face, the one he does when he thinks he's being clever: one eyebrow up, one down. He grabs his contaminated breakfast and plops it in the sink. While leaving the kitchen, he flashes another goofy face and smirky smile toward me.

Not fair! With this *Grace* information bomb whizzing clean over his head, Kiffer is the *lucky* one. So, he can starve to death—or not. I don't care.

But Grace? No way—the Old Lady can't be *my* grandma. Mom never talks about her, like, not ever. In fact, I never remember meeting her. So, what a surprise it was when Mom and Dad took Kiffer and me to her funeral some years ago. That morning, weirdness filled our house as we got ready for the two-hour trip. I've tried to forget this day and its long silent drive home after the ceremony. In the kitchen that same evening, Mom acted more zombie-ish than usual while chopping vegetables for a stew like a robot, and Dad downing foamy drinks the moment we got home while grumbling, "I wouldn't piss on her if she was on fire."

Hard to believe that from one slipped-out name, I learned more about Mom than from everything else I knew about her before tonight. Combined. *Did I mention how I feel about her stew? Double yuck.*

"It is true! Gramp, tell them," I say.

He sits, looking out the window. Since Gramp's stroke, his digestion has been tricky. After every meal, he sits in his chair next to the kitchen window to settle his stomach. If ever I needed a reaction from him, it's now. But I get nothing. He seems only interested in a woodpecker near the street, doing what woodpeckers do, pounding their brains out against a light pole, which now is exactly what I feel like doing.

I won't let this bird break my concentration—little as it is—not even if it would make a fantastic distraction. My mind stays focused on the night, rethinking everything that happened over and over. No way I can be wrong about all of this. I can remember every part. The boat, the magical bubbles, the mist. And especially the Old Lady.

But they don't believe me. A storm is ramping up inside me, the crazy kind. All the joints in my hands stiffen—my fingers flare out and press against the table as if it needs holding down to keep it from flying away. The muscles in my neck get so tight that my shoulders and elbows rise. This is where Gramp used to tell me to take a deep breath, count back from ten, then blow it all out. Ten, nine, eight . . .

With a sudden lurch, Gramp braces himself and gets up from the table. His chair screeches so loud that my hands jerk upward, and I hug my chest. He slides his bad leg under him, stands, and heads out of the kitchen. I sit motionless as the sound of his dragging foot stops behind me. His stillness lasts so long that I worry he's having another stroke. Before I can turn around to check, I feel a grip on my shoulder give a firm squeeze.

A calmness comes over me I can't explain. The entire night replays in my head, moment by moment. My shoulder gets released. I spin around and catch a glimpse of Gramp's blank face. He shifts his unbalanced weight and starts to stagger away. That feeling of being alone vanishes. Maybe the truth is, it doesn't matter who believes me if *I* believe me.

"Resume. Safe. Speed," he says, still looking forward.

"Gramp! You remembered!"

Jumping to my feet, I pounce in front of him. "You *do* remember!" Both corners of his lips—even the droopy side—curve into a tiny smile. I watch bright sparks ignite in his blue eyes. He gives me an impossible long wink. Within seconds, he collapses back into his empty stare, and with a few more drags from his foot, he slides out of the room.

I know what I saw—he winked; Gramp winked!

I stand in the kitchen, alone. But am I really alone?

Because of the night, I learned about things like filling moments. Maybe I get some of the extra love, protection, and understanding that my *blues* mom or my *hot-tempered* dad cannot give. Or from a silly brother, for that matter. Yep, I get it now. We all are connected, so we are never really alone.

My lips stretch so tight into the biggest smile that it feels as if they're going to split right in half. Gulping in the last of the soggy cereal, I throw my bowl in the sink and bolt out the front door.

Outside, I scan the street, looking for stray bubbles or boats. Nope, I didn't think I'd see any. Sounds of clanking bottles echo from the end of the block as the milkman finishes his route. Over by Mrs. C's house, an old man walks a dog. How funny the man's dressed, bundled in a raincoat, goulashes, and a raggedy umbrella. When he headed out for his walk, did he expect a tsunami? I let out a short, silly laugh. To see everything in the morning's sunshine makes it all feel different from last night, and yet, all the same. My heart feels so light.

After I confirm Mr. Shilaski's driveway is still empty, I plop down on our damp porch step. A tiny smile twitches into place as I look over the homes. And I do some thinking. And think. And think some more. I think about our neighbors: The loving Mrs. Dryver, the understanding sweet Mrs. C, and especially the always dependable superman Mr. Shilaski.

Then—like clockwork—here he comes, right on time. Mr. Shilaski's car passes by our house, turns into his driveway, and shuts off with a loud rumble.

It's time. My lips grow into a full-on grin. "Mom, gotta go see Mr. Shilaski!" I spring up and race toward his house.

Should I go over and say hi? There are no *filler* rules on how or what I should do to help him. Doesn't need to be, I guess. *Do kind things* is what the Old Lady said. And something else about sharks filling a glass? Ugh—I can't remember.

And you know what I think? It's going to be okay. I'm okay.

Maybe the truth is, it's what you have, not what you think you don't have, that's important. And my truth: I might not have everything, but I do have enough. I'm in the right family after all—every last one of them. Yep, in spite of everything, my complicated life fits me well.

From inside, I get no response back whatsoever. And just like that, some things don't change in my life, but some do. And someone—with an attention span of a gnat—most definitely did.

And it was all *Because of the Night.*

Acknowledgements

We are the sum of everyone around us. Some might calmly float in and stay, while others will storm-in and leave, but each quietly fill the holes our complicated lives create. I believe this to be my truth, so—it's with a deep gratitude, I want to acknowledge the following people. Each in their own way, refuse to let me tune out, detach, and move on…

To Jim—my true rock, who is a treasure beyond words.

To Mom, Dad & Mama Shirley, Grandma & Gramp L'Hommedieu, Mami & Papi Berrios—you taught me how to love.

To Matt, Latoya, Chris, David, Tim, Shawn, Julie, and Kim—who let me pour that same love into.

To Doug Raynor—who is the poor guy that knows Kiffer's pain firsthand.

To cousin Denise Picone—who is my lifeline for endless late-night edits and ever flowing blueberry wine.

To my dearest friend Jackie Hinoa—who's unconditional love inspires me daily to be a better person.

To Rajesh Gupta—who gives the purest critiques one could ever hope for.

To Hugh J. and Laura L.—who made me believe my words mattered. To Jason B.—who introduced me to the absolute-best music to write to … Classical!

To my dear buddy Bada-Bing—who always finds me when I'm lost.

To my cool Teamster brothers Steve Docherty & Tim Barker—who allowed me to join their crew on Amazing Stories—which is where the inspiration to write this adventure all began.

To Patti Fors—who's cheerleading spirit and kind friendship knows no limit.

To Kyra Nelson, Susan Van Appledorn, Gregory Fox, Sheryl Parbhoo, Rev. Jess Burton, Chris Mundy, Gabby Picone, Sosie Hublitz, Mollie Stallman, Cathy Webster, George Weinstein, & the Atlanta Writers Club —who are my wonderful beta readers, critiquers, & writing tribe.

And lastly, to Muse Literary. Thank you for believing in me—and most importantly—believing in Icky's story.

If I have forgotten anyone, please blame it on my head, not my heart.

About the Author

Rue L'Hommedieu, is a debut author, an active motion picture and television Teamster, as well as a lover of travel, old movies, and blueberry wine. Rue resides in the Southeast United States and is currently working on a second novel releasing in Fall 2023. Rue invites you to check out the website: www.ruebooks.com.